Foley's
Luck

Foley's
Luck

Stories by

Tom Chiarella

Alfred A. Knopf

New York

1992

THIS IS A BORZOI BOOK
PUBLISHED BY ALFRED A. KNOPF, INC.

Copyright © 1992 by Tom Chiarella

"Foley's Life Story" originally appeared in *Story* as "Berard's Life Story"; "Foley's Luck" originally appeared in *The New Yorker* as "Berard's Luck"; "Foley's Rapture" originally appeared in *The New Yorker* as "Berard's Rapture"; "Foley as Crabman" originally appeared in *The Florida Review* as "Berard as Crabman."

ISBN 0-679-40965-3
LC 92-53088

Manufactured in the United States of America

First Edition

For Winnifred and Angelo

Contents

Foley's
Luck

Foley's Escape Story

Dan's father drove the hearse straight by the main house and the barn. As they passed the house, a yellow light went on behind the curtains. It was then that Dan caught a glimpse of Marrissa Tamsley, who was in the sixth grade with him, standing in the window watching them like a silent, bony cat.

"She knows what we're here for," he thought to himself and that was his first real thought of the morning. Less than an hour before, when his father shook him, Dan had said "Hunting?" That was only a word, an instinct really, brought on by his father waking him so early, so abruptly. The half hour ride since then, slicing the drizzle and mist that blanketed the Saquoit Valley, had been a blank. Even so, he knew what they were here for. His mother had whispered it to him when she handed him his uncut slice of toast before they left. They were here for one of the Tamsley brothers. They were on removal.

★　　★　　★

He felt himself waking up a little and guessed that they were headed to one of the Tamsleys' other houses, a new one it seemed, since the road they were on was nothing more than two parallel ruts in the field. "Why didn't they bring him down themselves?" he asked. But his father concentrated on the road, which was slow going, and did not answer. They rocked along in the hearse for two or three hundred yards before his father brought it to a stop. "Now we walk," his father said. The road ahead was deep mud that the low-riding hearse could not handle without getting stuck. At the back of the hearse, they pulled out the shovels, the tool box and a large piece of canvas his father had stored under the gurney, and then began walking up the road. His father, carrying the canvas under his arm, a shovel over his shoulder, was quiet. Dan trailed, head down, carrying the tools and the other shovel, watching for dry places.

This was Dan's first removal. His father had always used Hank, Dan's older brother. Although he had no real idea why Hank wasn't there, Dan knew that his father was fed up with Hank. Hank was a tense subject in the family. There was a catalogue of things he did wrong. He drank. He disappeared for days on end. He ran his car off the road. He backed out of work at the funeral home.

While it was possible that his father had chosen to break in Dan on this particular morning, it didn't seem right that Hank wasn't there too. Their father was not much of a teacher and Dan had counted on his brother helping with the first few removals, offering pointers, providing warnings. But here Dan was, alone, trudging along behind his father, hoping he didn't make some incredible mistake. He tried to remember Hank's stories then, to call up his words.

"Nothing to it," Hank had once told him about removals. "There's nothing you don't already know." Dan hung on that now.

After half a mile, the road swung through a patch of young pines. Just beyond, the land rose up meanly in a large swath of wet earth stretching at least a quarter mile, from the forest on their left, down the slope, across what was once pasture, to a distant line of trees. The road ended abruptly at the wall of dirt in front of them. It was five feet high.

"Mud slide," Dan said softly.

His father looked up at the sky. "If it keeps raining," he said, "there'll be more of these."

"Have you ever seen a mud slide?" Dan said. "I mean while it's happening."

"Wouldn't want to," his father said, walking down the slope. "Look what it did to the house." He extended his arm straight out, pointing his shovel at the tree line. Dan couldn't see over the mud. He had the sensation that everything had been swallowed up, that he was looking at nothing, at a point where the sky simply butted up against the earth. Yet when he jumped he could see the peak of the house poking out of the mud in the distance. His father walked on ahead, picking up speed.

Dan started after him. The rain, which had fallen for weeks, hung like a sickness in the air. Now he could see the beginnings of a path where the grass had been trampled down by the Tamsleys on their trips out to this disaster.

Dan caught up. "Is it buried all the way?"

His father shook his head. "No, but it's pushed up against the trees pretty good."

They walked. Soon Dan felt the dampness seep into his boots. The world seemed out of scale. Next to him was a ridge of earth born only this morning. A mass of earth as

long and high as the ridge that ran behind his father's funeral
home, a ridge that Dan assumed had been there for centuries.
But this mass was new to the world, fresh and wet. He
wondered if it might still be moving, at a pace too slow to
detect. "This is just like the glaciers," he said out loud. "Or
like a river when you look at it from underground."

His father stopped. "What?"

"From underground," Dan said.

His father turned and looked at the mud slide, then
back at Dan. "What is it you're saying?"

"This looks like a river from underground," Dan said,
putting a hand out and twisting it over. "If you were standing underground. I mean completely upside down."

"What river? Where's the water?"

"If you were under it, Dad. Say the world were upside
down."

His father shook his head and put the shovel back over
his shoulder. "This is mud here, Dan," he said, looking
straight at him as if to make sure that Dan understood.

They walked a little farther and soon Dan could see the
house clearly. It was flipped up on its side, and the wedge
he had seen was not the peak of the house at all, but one of
the corners tilted and pushed against the trees. The front
porch lay splintered and crushed against a stand of young
birches. Dan felt almost as if he were looking at a normal
house from above. He decided not to mention this to his
father.

His father leaned in a window. "In here."

Dan moved alongside his father and looked in. The
room was hip-deep in mud that had poured in the window
from the top corner of the room. The bed stuck up at an
awkward angle. A lamp was pinned against the wall by the
dresser. Dan saw no body.

"Where is he?"

His father pointed to a patch of red in the mud just to the side of the bed. Dan squinted and began to see the slope of a human back. The red was a flannel shirt. "Why didn't they dig him out?" Dan said.

His father clumped the bag of tools up and into the window. "Why should they? That's what we do."

"How do they know who it is?" Dan said.

"This is Jimmy," his father said, lifting a leg up into the room. "It happened three days ago. They hadn't seen him in a couple of days, so they came out here and saw what happened. Even then, they didn't notice him at first." He pulled himself into the room and turned to help Dan. "Hand me my shovel," he said. "I wouldn't want them to dig him out. It's hard enough on people. That's what a removal is, Dan. It's my job."

Dan passed the shovel to his father and then climbed in behind him. His father placed one foot on the wall and one foot on the floor and began to gently dig away the mud, which had hardened around the body since the mud slide. Dan started in. "Dig a trench around him," his father said, "and we'll pull him out with the rope."

They dug for an hour. Periodically his father would sigh, raise a hand and stop to smoke a cigarette. He didn't say much to Dan, who watched the rigid shape of Jimmy Tamsley grow out of the hole they dug. As they broke the mud from his face, they found that his mouth was open, his eyes closed. His arms were frozen in front of him, bent inwards as if he were holding on to something big, like a tree. They broke as much of the mud away from his hair as they could. What was left formed a corona of blond hair and dark earth around his contorted face.

Dan had seen corpses all his life, so he didn't mind looking at Jimmy for long stretches of time. Jimmy never bothered him while he was alive, either. He had never really struck Dan as much more than an unlucky farmer in a valley of lucky ones; a lanky, dirty man, who paced the floors of Dan's mother's diner with a curious nervous energy, moving from booth to booth, seat to seat, in a clumsy attempt to pick up gossip and tips from the other farmers. Now, in this posture of death, trapped in the motion of escape, he seemed peaceful and Dan found himself staring.

When they dug down past the waist they found that he was naked below the red flannel shirt. Dan's father ran a rope down under the legs, but the mud at this lower level was still wet and wouldn't give. They pulled—his father heaving, the rope tied over his back like an ox—but the body would not come free.

So they dug. More slowly now, as they were tired and the space got tighter when they dug deeper. Soon they found that his calf was pinned underneath the bed, snapped in half, and it took them another hour to dig down under the bed to free it. Then the body came loose, and they lifted it with the ropes and rolled it to the window, where Dan pushed it out to his father.

They laid the body in the wet grass. It was late morning by then, the gray skies spread above them, the clouds higher than before. The mist had pulled up and away. His father reached down, stuck a finger in the mouth and pulled out a plug of dirt lodged in it. "Tamsleys might want to see him before we leave," he explained, wiping his hands on the canvas as he bent to wrap the corpse.

Dan threw the last flap over Jimmy Tamsley's broken, crouching body. One leg curled beneath the body, one leg— the broken one—was splayed out, so that Jimmy looked something like a dancer, arms frozen in embrace, hands clenching the hardened mud like a knife behind an unseen partner's back.

Dan's father pulled the flap back immediately. Dan

knew the tenor of the motion. His father had seen something he didn't like. "For the love of Christ," he said, throwing his cigarette to one side. "Will you look at this?" But he wasn't speaking to anyone in particular, Dan knew, only out loud. He reached down and pulled something like a belt that was wrapped around Jimmy Tamsley's waist. He pulled and yanked until the flaps of mud and grass that covered the groin and belly began to fall away. Dan reached in to pull at the dirt, but his father pushed his hands away. Soon Dan, standing at some distance now, could see that Jimmy Tamsley was wearing a leather harness, one that clamped his penis into a muddy hard-on. As his father cleared the last of the mud away, Dan stepped back a little. His father pulled a knife from the tool bag.

"What are you going to do?" Dan said softly.

"Jesus," his father said to himself as he knelt down next to the body. "Jesus, Jesus, Jesus." He slid the knife beneath the harness and began to cut it away. When the harness came free he carried it around the house and lobbed it up on top of the mud slide. Dan sat down on a birch tree bent under by the house, while his father resumed working, wrapping the corpse again. As he tied a rope around the bundle he said, with his eyes down, hands busy, as if talking to no one in particular, "No one should have to see that kind of thing." Then he signaled Dan to come around and lift with him. "No one should even have to know about it. Not me. Not you. No one."

He gave Dan a look then, a look that asked for a mutual understanding, a contract between father and son. "No one should know."

"I won't tell anyone," Dan said. "Don't worry."

His father walked back to the house and looked in the window at the ruined bedroom. Dan sat in the wet grass. "You could dig and dig," his father said, shaking his head.

Suddenly Dan knew. His father was looking for someone else, another body buried in the mud. It was as if a voice
were whispering in his ear, telling him things, showing him
the things he had never seen before. *A woman. They were doing
it. They were holding each other. Grabbing each other.*

Dan came up alongside his father. He scanned the room
from side to side. "I don't see anything," he said.

His father nodded. "Maybe there's nothing to see."

It took them more than fifteen minutes to drag the corpse
back to the hearse. By then it was past noon and his father
was anxious to get the embalmment underway. He pushed
the gurney to one side in the back and laid the body, wrapped
in canvas, on the floor. Then he backed the hearse out and
turned at the barn. He drove past the house without stopping. "They can see him after I get done with him," he said,
before Dan even wondered if that was the usual practice.

Dan could guess what the embalmment would consist
of. He had seen bits and pieces of these, and Hank had told
him the rest. They would hose the body off in the second
bay of the garage, which doubled as the spare embalming
room, then lift it onto the table in the real embalming room
and "blood" him. Embalming fluid would be pumped into
the carotid artery until it came out the jugular. Then the
joints would have to be broken, the limbs pushed into place.
The eyelids and mouth sewn shut, cotton balls pushed into
the ears. Makeup applied, a suit chosen, a casket.

Dan wondered about the hard-on, though. Hank told
him they sometimes had to cut them off. "Depends if it's an
open casket or not," Hank said. Dan felt sure that Hank was
teasing, although, as with everything about his father's business, he could never be sure.

Now they drove back across the valley and once again

they did not speak, though Dan, clearheaded now from the work and the long morning, knew there were things to talk about. He wanted Hank now. He had things to tell him. There were questions, real questions, to be answered.

His mother's diner sat in front of the lot on which their house stood. On the other side of the house was the funeral home and a small parking lot for the services. Beyond all this the valley fell away, pastures sloping into roads and lines of trees and then pastures again. As they pulled in, Dan saw his mother behind the counter, talking across the pass-through with Pete, the day cook. Hank's car was parked along the side of the diner. This made Dan happy, as he wouldn't have to do the embalming. The rest of the day would be his.

Once inside the garage, with the body on the table, Dan's father lit a cigarette and leaned on the edge of his equipment tray. "You must be hungry," he said, breathing out the smoke, which immediately filled the room with its smell.

"A little," Dan said. He was starving, but he didn't want to let on.

"Go get something to eat," his father said. "He can help me from here on out." Switching his cigarette from one hand to the other, he pointed an index finger straight up. His father meant Hank, and Dan could see that he had avoided using his name, but it seemed a good sign to Dan that his father wanted Hank to work at all.

"You did well, Dan," his father said, coughing a little as he exhaled. "You're a real Foley. A Foley can look anything straight in the face." He dropped his cigarette and stepped on it. "That's a hard thing to look at and you never flinched. That's good." Nodding to himself, Dan left.

He tried to think about what he had seen, but nothing registered. Jimmy Tamsley in a harness. The wall of mud. The chaos of the tilted bedroom. The other body, there and not there at the same time. He wondered briefly if there were mudslides in the Bible and made a note to check with his mother.

There were other questions too, but he wasn't sure now about what was secret and what wasn't. He couldn't tell his mother what he had seen. He needed Hank there to press him into the act of telling. Now he wanted to be sure of what he *shouldn't* know. Finding Hank was important.

"Took a long time," Dan's mother said when he came in the back door of the diner. She looked him up and down and Dan realized for the first time that his clothes were caked with mud. "Pretty rough?"

He sat down in a cane chair by the door. "There was a lot of mud," he said, picking at a clod stuck in the folds of his pants. "The whole house was on its side."

"You dug him out?" she asked. "Jimmy, right?"

Dan nodded, closing his eyes. He could smell tomato soup cooking on the stove. "You're hungry," his mother said as if he had held out his hands for food. Dan nodded again and she slipped a bowl off the top of the stack and ladled it full of soup.

"Where's Hank?" Dan said as she set the bowl down in front of him.

"He left," she said. "I'm not sure." She crumbled a stack of saltines and dropped them in the soup.

"You don't know where he is?"

"He left about an hour ago. He came in here drunk. He went out the back door of the diner," she said, brushing the crumbs on her apron. "He went I don't know where."

"What do you mean you don't know where?" Dan set down his spoon.

"Just what I said. I don't know where he went."

"What if he really left this time?" Dan said, standing.

His mother turned to the counter and began chopping vegetables. "I don't know," she said, looking out the window above the sink. "His car's still out there." Dan stared at the back of her dress. Finally she turned to him. "I don't know if he'll *ever* leave."

More puzzles. Dan couldn't figure what his mother meant by that. He left the kitchen without a word and hurried up to his bedroom to change. He wanted to go find Hank, who—he felt sure—was stumbling away from them out the flooded pastures that lay below the house. He might be leaving them for good, as he sometimes threatened to do. This might be his escape. But Dan would stop him. He could lead Hank back.

But when Dan walked into his bedroom, he immediately smelled Hank, who was lying in the bed, and felt his panic drop away. It was a stale smell, like dirty clothes, which he knew to be the alcohol on Hank's breath. On the chair next to Dan's desk was one of his father's legal pads on which Hank had started a letter. "Dear Dan, I got sick," it read, the sentence unfinished. Dan thought about shaking him awake, telling him to get downstairs, that he was needed.

He found himself speaking. "You should see what I saw," he said, barely aware of his own hope that Hank might roll over and open his eyes. "Hank," he said softly and then once again, louder this time, "Hank." But Hank was too drunk to wake up and give anything to Dan and Dan knew that. He wanted something simple—an explanation, a nudge, a joke. Anything that made things clearer and smaller.

He kneeled down on Hank's scattered clothes and leaned against the bed. Bending close to Hank, he listened to his breathing and became aware of the way Hank had fallen onto the bed—his head perfectly centered on the pillow, his hands joined, the stiff posture of his legs, the parting of his lips. Hank was unshaven. If Hank were a corpse, they would shave him, adjust him, fold him and unfold him until he looked just right, until he looked ready. That much Dan knew.

This man was his brother. This brother was a drunk, unable to take the burden of the morning from him, unable to laugh off the big things with Dan so that the small things might fall into place. Dan reached out and ran a hand along his brother's whiskers. Hank didn't stir. Soon, over Hank's soft, even breathing, he heard the rain begin again.

Then Dan could see himself, kneeling against the edge of the bed in his own dim room. He could hear his own words from a distance, telling the story of a morning. This is something ancient, he thought, something learned long ago.

Foley's Life Story

Foley often told the story of how he counseled his brother Hank to leave home for good. "He woke me," Foley liked to say. "I pushed up on an elbow. I saw right away that something was wrong." Often Foley took pains to set the scene—the early morning light through the dormer window, the distant clankings of the dairies all around them. "Hank's eyes were rheumy. His breath stank of bourbon." Hank, the story went, didn't know the way out. "I told him to leave," Foley said. "I told him to get the hell out."

That initial idea, the notion that Hank might want to tell someone he was leaving before he actually left, was a projection on Foley's part, a conjuring. Hank never came in, not even for a last look. So Foley never gave him any advice.

Besides that, most of his story was true. Hank was sloppy and he drank a lot; he disappeared for days on end, and when he was around he liked to fight, throw bottles, light fires where no one wanted them. By that point his father had pretty much cut him out of the family funeral home. No one knew where his money came from.

It was not always this way. Although he was fifteen years older than Foley, Hank had once been a regular brother in Foley's eyes. Hank taught him things. They had fished together, played hockey and board games. Yet by the time Foley was an adult, years after Hank had left for good, he had several different conceptions of his brother, each one tangled up in his mother, or his father, or the business, or himself. None of these was right, he knew. It seemed that he had told Hank's life story so many times, to so many people, that none of it was accurate anymore, none of it was true. Eventually Foley just gave up and tried, like his father, to forget about Hank altogether.

After his brother left, Foley took up solitary pursuits that made the absence all the more painful. He would trudge off alone through the wet grass to fish the creek south of their home. Late in the afternoon, he pitched Hank's ax against a telephone pole behind the funeral home. He could smell Hank—the metallic scent of Vitalis, the body odor of his familiar threadbare clothes. This perception of Hank's essence—around the corners of the house, underneath the basketball hoop, out ahead of him somewhere—led Foley to reshape his brother in his mind. That was the moment Hank became an idea—simply Foley's big brother, not Hank the drunk, Hank the layabout, Hank the fool.

Sometimes Foley continued with the story—largely true—of his parents' reaction to Hank's leaving. "They didn't seem surprised," he said. "He stole my mother's car and a load of groceries." His father took the whole thing with an elegance that was surprising, since he tended to fly into a rage over small things. But on the morning Hank left, only minutes after the reality had set in for Foley and his mother, his father simply walked into the kitchen, sat down, and asked, "Where's the Buick?"

"Hank took it," Foley's mother said.

"He's gone," Foley said, feeling desperately disconnected. "He left."

His father cocked an eye. "Where to?"

Foley and his mother spoke in unison then. "We don't
know." Their words fell into each other evenly. His father
stood and poured coffee. The sound was absurdly loud, tearing into the kitchen and the morning. Foley and his mother
said nothing. Taking their silence seriously, his father turned
back to them. "What? He left for good?"

Foley nodded. His mother stood, leaned past his father
for the coffeepot. "He took all the bacon," she said. "He's
gone."

"He's drunk," Foley's father said. "Or he was drunk."
He sipped his coffee and flipped to the box scores.

When he told this story, Foley always ended it this way:
"That was the last time he mentioned Hank for years." For
the most part that was true.

In college, at the University of Florida, at parties all flash
and murmur, bourbon and Coke in hand, it was often
brought up that Foley's father was an undertaker. Sometimes
Foley himself announced it. People cringed, but the questions always followed.

Foley answered them evenly, seriously. He did this to
counter the tone of the questions, the disdain for his father's
craft. His father had learned to embalm in mortuary school.
He had convinced Foley that there was a science to it. Foley
told, so that others would know. And people wanted to hear
things. The worst things. The hardest things. The biggest.
The bluest.

Foley often found himself unscrolling his childhood,
digging up stories, as a roomful of people waited. Truth was,
he didn't have many good stories. His father had held him

back from the business, pushing him toward college. Hank had always been meant to take over the funeral home. Since childhood, he had stood at his father's side during removals, embalmments, services. Hank always had stories. In Korea, he had worked in the mortuary division of the army at his father's insistence. Eventually Foley began to tell Hank's stories as his own. Punctured lungs. Severed arteries. Burns. When people asked questions, he thought fast, transforming Hank's war stories into car wrecks and farm accidents.

So how was this guy's arm blown off? (One of Hank's grenade stories.)

Dynamite. He worked in a quarry.

Were the eyes open or closed?

Open. They almost always are. (Hank's standard reply.)

What did it smell like when they found the body?

Just imagine. (Hank's favorite answer.)

In college an English teacher asked him to write his life story in a thousand words. His perception of his own childhood changed. There were distortions throughout the whole paper. "I was born in upstate New York." (The teacher wrote in the margin: Where? Specifically.) "My father is an undertaker and a dairy farmer." (Once, for a year, they had three cows.) "My mother runs a diner." (It was closed. This too had been short-lived. The house specialty was something his father called "Half-dollar doughnuts." Glazed doughnuts cut in half and toasted. They never really caught on.) "My older brother is an engineer." (A lie.) "My father owns 200 acres of farmland." (Twenty.) "I wrestled at 157 pounds in high school." (118 pounds.)

To his mind these were mere factual tinkerings. But he went further with his "memories." Although he never played baseball, and knew very little about it, he wrote: "We live only a mile from the ballyard, and it seems that I spent most of my childhood at the hot corner." Of his bedroom, which had one window facing the funeral home parking lot, he wrote: "My room has bay windows, facing west, which afford me a fine view of our cozy valley. Many nights I fell asleep watching the sun set slowly in the west."

It irked him that the teacher gave him a C. "You ignored your father's job," she wrote, "and in so doing missed out on your best material. An undertaker must have a lot of interesting stories."

One summer his mother showed him a letter from Hank. It was the only one she had received. Postmarked Illinois, it was over a year old when she showed it to Foley. In that time, she had taken to referring to Hank's absence as his "adventure." The letter was short, full of hellos to everyone and very little else. After Foley finished reading it, he laid it flat on the kitchen counter. "When I opened it," his mother said, "this fell out." She handed him a photograph: Hank lying on a cot. He wasn't wearing a shirt.

"It looks a lot different there," his mother said, although he couldn't see how she got any notion of "there." The only thing Foley could glean about "there" was that the window next to Hank's bed, if indeed it was Hank's bed, was cracked and the walls were knotty pine. Nevertheless the letter had seemed to settle his mother. "He needed to go west," she said. "He had that in him." To Foley that sounded a lot like gobbledegook, the stuff of literature.

Before Hank was shipped to Korea, he used to babysit Foley, who vaguely remembered an afternoon when Hank let him chew on a bullet. Other than that, Foley's first memory of

Hank involved his brother's stiff presence during the services at the funeral home. Hank was constantly in the background at these ceremonies, his tie slightly askew, pulling at his coat to get it to sit just right, as out of place as any first-time mourner. Hank's manner was a source of tension with their father, who spent years trying to round him into shape. Foley once heard his father shouting at Hank from behind a closed door: "You walk around like everything is your fault!"

Not true. Even as a boy Foley knew that. Hank blamed no one, and took no blame either, for his troubles. Upon returning from Korea, Hank made plenty of references to "the fates." He blamed everything on them—his failure in school, his drinking, his restlessness and short temper.

The first time Foley heard about Hank's "fates" he was nine, on a morning when Hank was keeping an eye on him for their mother. They sat together in Hank's tiny house. It was what his mother called a railroad shack—three rooms, all in a row, small windows, low ceilings. Foley sat and flipped through Hank's comic books, as he had a hundred times before. It was a rainy, sleet-driven day. He was about five miles from home.

Hank spent the morning stacking spent shell casings. They were brass and steel, tall as bowling pins. Hank had brought back a duffel bag full of them from Korea. Other vets, the boys returning to the valley, had brought small horses made of glass, rough bells from China, things to roll from palm to palm. Hank brought nothing, save the shell casings and his fatigues. No souvenirs, no presents for the family. When he set the shell casings on the kitchen table for the first time, it was done with a sense of ceremony. Their father was stunned. "That's it?" he said. "That's what you brought back to us?"

Hank laughed and held up a shell casing. "These things are beautiful. They're like art," he said. "I'll shine them up and you'll see."

Foley, like his mother and father, was baffled. Later he heard his mother talking to Hank in the kitchen. "No photographs, Hank?" she said. "Couldn't you at least have brought pictures of your friends?"

Hank mumbled then, something about too many friends. "We're planning a reunion. I'll be getting letters." Foley heard that for years, but he never believed it. No letters ever came.

On the morning when Hank brought up the fates, he stacked the casings in a pyramid, then laid them flat out, end to end, like a snake. Foley knew this was supposed to be babysitting on Hank's part, but his brother seemed to get a charge out of treating Foley like an adult. Foley went along with it happily. Hank had already let him smoke two of his Camels and had given him a cup of coffee. From the couch, he watched Hank stack and restack. He was queasy.

Hank lifted his hands slowly from a column of casings stacked three high. He was sitting cross-legged on the floor and, as Hank held his hands still like that, Foley thought it looked as if he were performing a magic show.

"Dan," Hank said, "do you ever think about the fates?" Hank kept his hands poised, his eyes on the task.

Foley had heard Hank say, "Do you ever think about the face?" Thinking that it might be something from Korea, he said nothing.

"You know, the forces that control everything," Hank went on. "Who lives, how they live, what they run into, when they die."

Even as Foley was drawing up his vision of this face— the face, he assumed, of God—Hank kept on.

"You could die in your sleep," he said. "Or a plane could fall out of the sky and crash right into your living room."

"It could?"

"Oh sure," Hank said. "It happens. Not a lot, but it happens."

Even at nine years old, Foley had heard a lot about death. It hardly puzzled him. But this thing about a plane crashing into the living room scared him. They might be in there, listening to the radio when it happened. All of them. His mother, too.

Up to now, he had seen death as something benign, something that dwelled somewhere clean and warm. The kitchen, he realized. His family talked about it there over dinner—spooning out peas, refilling the iced tea—nearly every night. They were somber, to be sure, but no one in the kitchen—not his mother, certainly not his father, not even Hank—ever seemed afraid.

The face was a new element. Foley quickly erased the face of God. The beard, the wizened eyes, dropped away. It was a big, pale face, he decided, as big as a state—Rhode Island, perhaps—as blue and cold as lake ice.

Hank turned and went into the kitchen. "You want some toast?" he said.

After a moment, Foley followed. When he turned the corner, Hank was standing in front of the open icebox, a piece of bread in one hand, tipping back a bottle—rum, Foley thought—with the other. He drank in great gulps. It dripped down his chin.

"Hank," Foley said, "what does the face look like?"

Hank jumped. "Jesus, Danny!" He looked at the bottle as if he were surprised it was there. He wiped his chin with his sleeve, then let his arm fall. Tilting his head, he paused a moment. "Dad hit me, you know," he said. "All the time."

What Hank had said didn't surprise Foley. Truth was, he had seen his father hit Hank once in the funeral home parking lot. Something was yelled about the hearse, then Foley heard the word "belt" or "felt" and then, just as Hank threw up his hands and turned away, his father decked him. Foley remembered thinking that it looked like a punch from a cowboy movie, clean and quick across the back of the head. Hank went down hard.

What Hank was saying in the kitchen that day was "Dad hit me *and not you*." Foley could see that, but he didn't know what to make of it. He expected that when the time came he'd get hit too.

After a minute Hank buttered a slice of bread and slid it in the broiler for toasting. Nothing more was said about fate.

Two weeks later their father had them working, pulling stumps at the edge of a small pasture about a quarter of a mile from their house. Hank had showed up late, and their father grumbled for an hour or two, but the three of them had pulled five stumps and were making good time for the most part. They had a tractor with a long steel cable, several axes and iron bars.

The face had been in Foley's head for a day or two after Hank had told him about it. After one particularly bad dream, in which he saw the face in several windows all at once, he went to his mother and asked her about it. She soon figured out his mistake. "I think Hank meant fates, honey." And she took some time to explain what she knew of them. She told him that he didn't have to worry about them. "They aren't worth it," she said. Foley took much comfort and was able to pretty much forget about the face because the weather suddenly turned for the better. Outside, with the sky like blue enamel, the face, the fates, hardly seemed a factor.

"Get behind this, Dan," Foley's father said at one point. Foley went to the spot where his father stood and leaned with him against an iron bar wedged in behind a stump.

They had run the cable underneath the stump and Hank was running the tractor, pulling from the other side.

"Rock it, Hank," their father yelled. With the engine revving, Hank couldn't hear him. He held his open hand next to his ear and tilted his head to say so. "Rock it!" their father yelled again. Then he walked around to the other side of the stump, grabbed hold of the cable and pulled with the motion of the tractor, which Hank soon took to rocking.

After a minute of this, the cable snapped. It coiled around their father's arm and the motion of the tractor jerked him back flat on his back. Foley shouted and Hank immediately cut the engine.

Their father was cut, cleanly and deeply, from the wrist around to the back of his elbow and then again, very badly, at the shoulder. His arm was clearly broken in at least one place, bent just above the elbow. "Get me on the tractor," he said.

It suddenly seemed to Foley that they were all shouting, but in truth Hank was the only one who spoke. He moved quickly, fluidly. He pulled a plastic raincoat out of the tool box and wrapped it around his father's arm without seeming to hurt him. He tied the arm off at the shoulder with a length of cord, produced magically from the pocket of his jeans. The whole time he worked, he spoke rhythmically and mechanically to both Foley and his father. "Don't worry, don't worry, don't worry." His hands flashed from one job to the next. Soon he reached down and scooped up his father gently. Foley did what he could, lifting the heels of his father's shoes.

Hank put a foot on the axle of the tractor, then, stepping up, set his father down on the hood. He set Foley up next to him and told him to hold down the artery under his father's armpit. "Don't let go," he yelled. "Not even if he begs you."

Foley pinched hard on his father's arm and prayed that there would be no begging. He knew he couldn't take that. Hank moved them swiftly back to the house. After a moment of bump and jostle, their father was calm. He spoke to Foley once. "You're doing well," he said. After that Foley could hear him whispering to himself. "It burns, it burns, it burns." Later on, he realized that his father was talking about the heat of the engine beneath them.

Years later, when Foley told this story, he always took a few minutes to dwell on the two weeks that followed the accident. His father recovered. The cuts were deep, but the break was clean and easy to set. His father spent twenty-two days in the hospital, with his arm suspended beside him. Foley and Hank were lauded in the local paper as heroes, mentioned by name at the church service, and asked time and again to tell the story from beginning to end. To Foley it seemed to be an extended holiday. Meals were brought to them at all hours by different neighbors, snug in baskets, still warm in casseroles. He was shuttled back and forth from the hospital, where he sat with his father and read the sports page aloud to him, and then to their house, where he worked with Hank to keep things going, then back to the hospital again.

It surprised everyone that Hank's smooth, informed behavior carried over into the next few weeks. He covered for his father at the funeral home, and did so without embarrassing anyone, ordering supplies, keeping the books, tuning the hearse. To Foley, the world seemed in balance.

When their father returned, things slipped back. He found several things wrong with the way they had kept the funeral home. "That hedge is too high," he said, standing in the parking lot, his arm in a cast that stuck straight out from his shoulder. Inside he fussed about the arrangement of chairs, the order of the instruments, the state of his office. "Good Lord, Hank, can't you see the way we've always had it?"

Their father's arm grew stronger and after a year he was proud to tell anyone who would listen that he could bend it fully. "It's stronger than it ever was." Hank became his old self—hungover or drunk, late or altogether absent. Things went on this way. As the arm grew stronger, Foley's mother once noted, Hank got weaker.

Some fifteen years later, having just settled into his first full-time job as a draftsman, Foley realized that his mother had been oversimplifying. It was often suggested over the years— by Foley's friends, his cousins, his grandmother, and later by his wife—that his father had driven Hank away. There was truth in this, he knew, but it was not in and of itself a truth. The two of them were not so much opposed as they were connected.

He remembered that after the accident his father would describe Hank's reaction in this way: "He did it just the way I would have. It was like I was doing it to myself. Very smart, very calm." He said this many times over, often in Hank's presence, meaning it as a compliment to his good sense, his basic instincts. After a while Foley could see Hank's face go blank when the story started up.

Before Hank left home for good, he made a campaign of not washing, so that his father wouldn't use him for removals or services. He was driving himself from them, Foley later realized. "I must have been the only one that didn't see it," he told a friend. "It was like a ritual, but I was oblivious to it. The only thing that surprised me was that he actually smelled. I told him that, and he laughed."

Hank had put his hand on Foley's shoulder, a gesture

he had never made before, not that Foley could ever remember anyway. "That's the idea, Dan," he said. "I'm trying to control the fates."

At the time, Foley accepted this statement with the strange assurance that it meant something. Years later he would realize that his awareness grew like a fingernail, which he bit back constantly in puzzlement. "You don't want to take over the home, do you," he said to Hank.

Again Hank laughed. "I don't want to be Dad," he said. "And I don't want him to be me. Nobody is me."

Again Hank had left something unsaid. Foley wanted to complete it for him: "Nobody is me, *but me.*" Then he wanted Hank to complete it himself, so that things might make sense. Foley thought for a long time that he needed to get Hank to say it again, the unfinished part anyway, but Hank never did.

When Foley finally admitted to his mother that Hank had never said good-bye to him, he was almost forty-five. The story about him sneaking into his room early in the morning was a lie.

"I know," his mother said. They were on a jet at the time, flying north. His mother had a plastic cup full of white wine on her tray table. Foley had rum. He was stunned.

"You've listened to that story for all those years," he said.

"That was your story," she said. "I have mine."

She touched him on the wrist. "Actually he said good-bye to me. Early in the morning, just like you always said."

Foley nodded. "Is that true?"

His mother laughed. "I don't know," she said. "But I gave him all those groceries. Every stinking thing in the refrigerator. I emptied it with him, put it all on the back seat of that old car. He may not have said good-bye, not out loud, but I knew what was happening."

"Why did you let me get away with that story?"

"I don't know," she said again. "I used to think you needed a hero, a big brother." She sipped her wine and stared straight ahead. "You've done all right without one, though. I was probably wrong."

For a long while, when people asked, Foley had echoed Hank's words about himself by saying, "My brother is a nobody." After that he told people he was an only child. Then he went back to the more complex stories. His brother was an engineer, a gambler, a tax consultant, a criminal, a liar. Recently he had been telling people his brother was dead.

Now, on this plane, with his mother right next to him, he saw the old vision of Hank, preparing to leave, creeping around the house, the early morning light at work in the windows. He was drunk, most likely, or working one off. And happy. This time when he said good-bye, as they tossed food—the mayonnaise, the applesauce—into the back seat, it was final. And yet, as always, this vision brought on another for Foley, the one of Hank at the wheel of the tractor. The Hank of his own making, the soldier, the brave spirit, gearing the tractor up in the flat spots, slowing to cross the furrows. Then his face was steady and calm, eyes fixed beyond them—his father and little brother—on the horizon. Foley saw himself then too, crouched on the hood of the tractor, his father's blood running out over his fingers. But he felt okay. Hank was there. They were moving. With this story, he slept.

Foley's
Confessions

One summer, long and Florida heavy, I decided to become a bad person. I went to St. Petersburg, took an apartment and found a job in a movie theater that faced the beach. That was neither the start of it nor the end of it. It's only what I choose to open with. This story closes with an angry theater owner holding a gun to my head.

I made the decision the night after I was blackballed by a fraternity at the University of Florida. I'm not suggesting cause and effect here either, only that another life occurred to me that evening, one that I had never considered for myself. I could split myself, become someone new, someone dangerous—the skulking kid with the boxed Pall Malls, the one who hung smoke rings and whirled into the night. I knew the decision was juvenile, that I would be minor-league bad. But my path had been chosen. I went ahead: brooding, drinking, skulking.

I was far from my family and I soon found that no one cared if I didn't shave, or if I missed class. Late one evening I punched out a window. That was the best I could muster.

I grew comfortable with all of this. When the time came to go home for the summer—north, to my mother's questions, to my father's business—I decided that I needed distance and went off by myself, south, to St. Pete. I took a one-room unfurnished apartment above a drugstore and got a job at a theater—the Beach Cinema—only a block away. There was sand everywhere in the apartment; I could see the Gulf from my fire escape. The world took on an air of finality.

I had brought with me a duffel bag of clothes, which I lived out of for the summer. In it was a box containing my initiation sweatshirt, with Greek letters stitched across the front. We had been allowed to order these things, but not to wear them—not until we became brothers. Soon after arriving in St. Pete I opened the box, pulling the tissue paper back, like the sheets of a marriage bed, to take a look at the sweatshirt. I could have resold it back at school, but that morning I took out a double-edged razorblade, and began to cut away the letters. There was no plan; I just wanted them gone. I took off two of the letters and left the B—a beta—which I thought was puzzling enough to be left by itself. It stood for nothing. I had simply castrated the shirt. I wore it day after day.

The section of St. Pete where I lived and worked was known as Redington Beach. There was not much to it in those days—just Gulf Boulevard, a strip of shops built on the edge of a swamp, a dock on the inlet, a post office and the Beach Cinema. People—from places like Minnesota and Wisconsin—were building tiny bungalows all along the empty grid of streets. Someday these numbered streets would be jammed full of houses, but now they were vacant lots, cleared and ready. On the south side, the point where the township blurred into Madeira Beach, someone had posted a sign that read REDINGTON BEACH—PREPARED FOR PROGRESS. At the other end there was another sign: REDINGTON BEACH—CITY OF THE FUTURE. I found disagreement on the motto, but everything there pointed forward.

For an architecture student like myself it should have been heaven. There were jobs galore—as surveyors, carpenters, laborers, electricians—but I liked the submerged quality of life at the movie house. Even as I intently watched the buildings go up, I feigned lack of interest and told phony stories of how I once stole cars.

I fancied myself living incognito. No one there knew my past; no one was much connected to my present. I took a post office box. My parents had no idea where exactly I lived. I had no phone. It drove my mother to tears.

I worked for a man named Rudolph Korn, who owned the theater and several lots nearby. I assumed he had plenty of money since his taste ran toward the rare. He drove a Mercedes, a truly foreign car in those days, and collected an assortment of exotic fish, which he kept in recessed, wall-length tanks at the theater. After he hired me, he gave me the tour of the theater. Stopping at the tanks, he ran a finger along the bottom of one and said, "These are meant for effect. To make people feel tropical. Movies should be like a vacation, right?"

Rudolph had thick arms and a stomach that looped out over his belt like some giant gland. He wore a sad, untrimmed mustache and liked to let the beard around it grow for three days at a time before shaving. He favored doubleknits, in various shades of white (which he liked to call "buff"). When I first met him, I thought he was sick, but I later realized that he was pasty by nature. I think he was forty-three.

He hired me, and I was grateful. He had several University of Florida students working for him, most living at home for summer vacation. Among them was a nineteen-year-old girl, named Grace McBride, to whom he was rumored to be engaged. Grace worked at the ticket window. I started as an usher, but moved up quickly to the concessions stand—the Snack Bar, as Rudolph called it. He claimed he had invented the term.

Rudolph kept me away from the concessions stand until I agreed to try to look happy. When I did work there, I was without shame. I stole and stole and stole. Opening boxes of candy, I ate a few pieces, then resold the box even as I chewed on my third nougat. I devised systems to circumvent Rudolph's inventory—restacking used popcorn boxes in among the new, substituting counterfeit drinking cups for the real thing. I pocketed an extra ten dollars a night.

There were other rituals, just as mean-spirited as my stealing. After clocking out, I liked to watch the end of the late show while taking short pulls of Jim Beam. The theater was mostly empty. I sat in the back, with my feet up, laughing out loud in all the wrong places. Occasionally someone would stand up, or walk back, and ask me politely to shut up. Rudolph never got wind of it.

As I've said, all of this was a pose. I knew that even then. But I began to feel that I was almost dangerous. The detachment from my former lives—the one in Gainesville and the one before it in upstate New York—was what I liked. I rarely called my parents that summer and wrote no letters. With no one to talk to, I walked constantly—not often on the beach, more often along the streets of the undeveloped township, listening for the sound of people's radios, for the old Minnesota men on their new electric organs.

⋆   ⋆   ⋆

I was heartsick for Grace after the first week. This threw my planned isolation out of whack, since all I really wanted was to be with her, happy or sad, clothed or naked—and this required extensive talking and a general curiosity, both of which violated the discipline I'd set up for myself.

The first time I met Grace was on the sidewalk outside the theater, just before it opened one afternoon, as we waited for Rudolph to unlock the doors. She had just been to the beach and I could see beads of sweat forming on her skin.

I said nothing to her, staring straight out at the water as if it held some message for me. Then Grace introduced herself. "What's the B stand for?" she asked, nodding at my sweatshirt, at my chest.

As I looked down, I thought about the possibilities. I wanted to say something dark, something scary, but I could only come up with "bird" and "bench" as these were the only B words in my line of vision. I lied. "It stands for Barnes," I said. "That's my name." She nodded. "It's what people call me. Just Barnes."

She called me Barnes that whole first night, apparently thinking that it was my first name. Even when I told her the truth—that my name was Dan Foley—I did so with a lie at the ready. I was changing my name, I would tell her; I was in the middle of a painful split with my family. I braced myself when I told her, somehow expecting that she would care, that she would even be angry when I told her the truth, but when I said "Foley," she only smiled.

"Pretty name," she said, trying it out for herself. "Foley," she said. "Foley." She called me only that from then on. Even after she found out that other people called me Dan, she rarely called me anything else. I loved it.

★   ★   ★

When Grace sat at the ticket counter I watched her back. I loved her straight spine, her slender shoulders. When she was next to me, doling out popcorn, I caught little whiffs of soap. Once I asked about her relationship with Rudolph—were they engaged?—but she laughed and said nothing. I was left to figure.

I began to watch Rudolph's hands, picturing his soft palms, his many-ringed fingers, cupped around one of Grace's breasts. In this vision, the two of them met at one of the beach motels—The Galleon, The Tides, The Ship's Mate—while I prowled the streets, looking to bust in and end it all.

Once Grace claimed she was worried about Rudolph. He had openly wished for cancer. I pshawed and dug into the mound of popcorn.

"He said, 'Cancer. I want it.' " She looked earnest, concerned. "Those were his exact words."

I was hitting off a box of Whoppers stashed under the cash drawer. I popped one in my mouth and took an order. "Rudolph is morbid, Grace. Don't let it get to you." For the moment, I wanted yet another persona; I tried out the sensible, stalwart Foley. "I'll talk to him if you want."

"You don't have to sit there with him every night like I do. He's so dark, Foley. It rubs off."

I took another Whopper in my mouth, crunched down on it and sucked until it dissolved. "Try getting him angry," I said, casting a glance at the office door. "Get the life force flowing." That was the best advice I could come up with.

She was not consoled. I spent the rest of the night wondering where the two of them went together and what it was they did. He took her to dinner, I guessed, to the expensive Cuban restaurants in Tampa or to swarthy Eastern

European spots, where everyone's arms were as thick as his. In those places he talked low and suicidal to her.

I now think it's funny that I never tried to figure out Rudolph's death wish. I couldn't appreciate the subtleties of motivation and I didn't try. Nothing seemed explainable.

More importantly, Grace kissed me quite suddenly on the beach that night. I began to learn that she liked to take giant leaps, with or without me. We said nothing to Rudolph.

We began to go to dinner together, but more often we walked the beach, despite my passion for roaming the streets. "There are palmetto bugs running all over the pavement at night," she said. That's what she called roaches. All Floridians did as far as I could tell.

Sometimes we ended up in a clinch, on the beach if the tide was low, or in her apartment. I loved the feel of her dresses against my chest. The buttons, the pins, the edges of her pockets. I tried my best to be a gentleman—yet another version of myself, my new night persona—and did not rush her. Once I got my hand up under her skirt, where I brushed the inside of her thigh. She took a deep breath and said "Thank you" as if I had just told her I liked her new hairdo. I pulled my hand back immediately, figuring she was betting on my honor.

She kept seeing Rudolph, though, and it ate at me that Grace wouldn't tell me what they did together. I asked if she loved him. Again she laughed. "It's nothing like that," she said. "He's harmless."

Once, a long time after all of this, I recounted this story to Grace and she remembered saying, "He's harmless. It's you

I love." But I cannot say I have any memory of her saying this, nor can I figure out why she loved me so quickly, so surely. "At first you seemed scary," she told me once. "Then I realized you weren't anything to be scared of. I liked it that way."

One night Rudolph and Grace left me to close the theater by myself. We had a particularly long movie showing, one that took place in France and involved knives. Grace knew it drove me crazy that she still went out with Rudolph, especially since I had begun touching her breasts, but she reassured me. "Only a week or two more," she said. "Then we'll be done."

When they left that night Grace shot a knowing smile over her shoulder at me, Rudolph waved merrily and I was suddenly alone.

Leaning out the door, I watched them turn off the boulevard a few blocks down. They were moving toward Rudolph's house.

I checked the ticket count. In the theater behind me, there were thirteen people, watching the last thirty-five minutes of the show. I could duck out, follow Grace and Rudolph for a block or two, and still get back before the credits. At the very least I'd know if they ended up at his house.

So I locked the cash drawer and the office, leaned out the glass doors, looked around as if someone might see me— as if someone might care—and took to tracking them.

But there was no adventure in the chase. They ended up at Rudolph's house, as I'd suspected. I watched them through the blinds, which were only half drawn. Grace walked in, took off her clothes and sat in a large hammock. Rudolph backed away, opened a closet, wheeled out an easel and began to paint.

★   ★   ★

The saltiness of the place began to overwhelm me as I stood there, in the night air, with my hands pressed to Rudolph's stucco. Everything was covered with salt—the windowsill, the streetlamp, the palm leaves, the cinder-block retaining walls, my hair, my shirt, my bow tie. I had climbed through it to this spot. Now I felt heavy and slow, glued there, at the window, by the sight of my Grace and by the warm salt air.

I remember thinking how I might confront Grace with my newfound knowledge. "I'm not even angry," I would begin. That was true. I felt lucky; I was seeing her naked. So ran my general spirit that night. I stood there, as close as I dared, watching for a full twenty-two minutes before sprinting back to the theater. I arrived, breathless, to meet the last of the customers on their way out. They shot me queer glances as I ran up to them. "Sorry," I panted, waving good-bye. "Raccoons. Raccoons in the garbage." That just came to me.

I've often tried to think of adjectives to describe the way Grace looked that night. At the time I settled on "innocent" and "beautiful." These were much like those B-words I came up with earlier—the first things in my line of vision. Years later, with Grace at my side, when I told this story at parties, I used words like "majestic" and "stately." She said that I made her sound like a cruise ship. Now I just say she looked "good" and that the sight of her like that—lounging, flipping through a magazine—was "welcome."

I remember that the blinds afforded me a partial view, so that I had to change my perspective to see each part of her body. I got good at it, though, because I was there every night that week.

I didn't say anything to Grace about my discovery. I

just begged out of several dates, in hopes that she might see Rudolph even more. She did. He was finishing his painting. I could see that from the window.

Each night I cut it closer and closer on the sprint back to the theater, until it finally occurred to me that I hardly needed to be there at all as the people filed out. At the drug-store below my apartment, I bought a tiny sign that said THANK YOU, which I propped up on the snack bar before I left each evening. I began to stay later at the window, prop-ping my ass against a pawpaw tree, until I finally didn't worry at all about returning.

One evening the moon was out, full and glassy white over the Gulf, and I got worried that someone might see me there at the window of Rudolph's house. So I left a little earlier than I had the night before, still long after the end of the late show, and walked back to the theater along the beach. It was late August and the night was as hot as they get.

Grace had taught me to like walking by the water. She pointed out the things one couldn't see in the darkness, as well as the many things—the shells, the weeds, the debris—that became visible as I walked over them. That night I could see as far out as I ever had before. A lighted boat and not much else bobbed on the horizon. There was plenty out there, I knew.

I missed Grace and wanted her then. We had recently agreed to see more of each other when we returned to school in the fall. I had decided to tell her I knew about the painting. I would say, "I accept it. I respect it." This was yet another Foley. Honest Foley. Tolerant Foley. Good Foley.

When I turned off the beach, I could see right away that something was wrong inside the theater. Things looked wavy and out of balance. At first I thought someone had

turned off a bank of lights in the lobby, but as I ran up to
the doors of the theater, I found that the sidewalk was wet,
as if someone had run a hose over it.

The lobby was flooded. The surface of the water shone
with broken glass, popcorn and boxes of candy. In this mess,
in the glint of broken glass, the patterns of jujubes, I could
see the tiny splashes of Rudolph's dying tropical fish from
one end of the lobby to the other.

At that point I was struck with a queer sensation, a little
like being kicked in the neck. This sensation told me I had
finally made it. I was bad.

After all the phone calls were made, after the police had come
and gone and the cleanup had begun, Rudolph called me into
his office to hear my story one more time. I was so far past
sorry that I didn't care. The lobby had been demolished. Fire
extinguishers emptied, snack bar smashed, cash drawer jim-
mied, fish tanks shattered with Rudolph's very own ball-
peen hammer. I thanked God that I had left the projection
room locked.

When he sat, Rudolph took a deep breath. I suddenly
saw him as very old, like a grandfather is old. He had a bottle
of scotch on his desk. He told me to sit and did not offer me
a drink.

"How could you not have heard?" he said. "This is like
a war happened in here." He leaned back in his chair. I told
my story again: I had been up in the projection room, cleaning up after the show. I'd forgotten to lock the doors before
I went back up.

"Four thousand dollars' worth of fish," he said. He held
up four fingers. "Four thousand."

I shook my head. "I'm sorry." I was trying so hard to
radiate sincerity that I could see myself—as if from some

corner of the room—shaky, alone, nervously gripping the arms of the chair.

Rudolph got up then and closed the door to the office, and that's when he pulled the gun. I didn't see when he picked it up, but I felt it because he came up behind me, jerked me into a half nelson and pressed the barrel end of it against my temple. It felt absurdly big, as if the tip were the diameter of a doughnut. I cried out.

"Do you think she didn't know you were at the window?" he whispered. "Do you really think I didn't know you were there?"

"I wasn't," I said. He choked me. I put my hands in the air, a criminal now, or a victim. I couldn't tell the difference. He pulled tighter.

"Liar!" he said, twisting me a little. "She saw you!"

"I wasn't," I said, pulling at his arm. "It wasn't me! I don't know what you're talking about." I could hear him grinding his teeth.

He loosened a little and I bent my head to one side and slipped out. I turned to him. The gun was down. "It was you at the window," he said. "She saw you tonight."

"No," I said. "Not me."

"She told me you were there," he said. "I was going to go out and get you, but she said no. She said it was okay."

I wondered again when he had picked up the gun, thinking, If he'd had it while he was painting, he could have shot me through the window. I heard what he said about Grace seeing me at the window. It didn't register. I was too busy believing that I hadn't been there. He said nothing for a moment, then stared past me, as if he was reading a map on the wall. "I presume you know that you're fired," he said. I nodded, and then he slapped me.

*   *   *

I was the first person to ever split a movie theater. At least I thought of the idea. For a while I made a good bit of money doing it. My architectural firm called it "theater conversion." We built soundproof walls down the middle of old theaters, split their giant screens and realigned the seats as best we could. Theater owners loved it, since it doubled the draw overnight. Once, in a local paper, my firm was credited with "the death of the double feature."

The idea for splitting occurred to me the night Rudolph held a gun to my head. It happened like this. After he slapped me, he told me to get my things and go. It was numbingly quiet as I walked through the theater, down the aisle toward the locker room. My face was still burning, my ear still ringing. In among the seats I saw empty popcorn boxes—here and there, the random drinking cup. The vandals hadn't come in here and this part of the world seemed normal. Things could be picked up, the floor could be swept, the reels rewound and things would start again tomorrow. Like normal. The lobby, where Rudolph sorted through the wreckage and wept, was a ruined place, another world really, separated from this one only by a wall, by a line. One place, two worlds. Like that.

I had crossed lines again and again all summer. All I wanted that night was to stumble out, find my way back, recross that line, march along it for the rest of my life. This was the good-bad line I was thinking about. But as I kneeled to pick the last of my stolen change from the floor of my tiny locker, I wasn't sure that I'd be able to move ever again. So I knelt there for a long time, rattling nickels in the palm of my hand. I now recognize it as an attitude of prayer.

I didn't see Grace again until I got back to school, and even then she wouldn't talk to me. From the moment I saw her in the doorway of the biology building, I wanted to tell her everything. Not just about watching in the window, but everything—the stealing from the till, my summer-long callousness. Without hoping for more, I wanted her to know.

To her credit, she wouldn't have it. She refused my phone calls, left my letters unanswered and turned away whenever I approached.

Finally, after a year, I saw her at a party in New York of all places. I worked then at a Manhattan architectural firm, keeping my theater conversion idea very close to the vest. I had a decent, windowless office that I shared with an older student from Cornell. That firm had the first electric pencil sharpener in New York City.

I saw Grace as she came in, but avoided her, as she was with a date. Between drinks I reminded myself to get her phone number. "Are you in New York now?" I would say, just as casual as that.

But before I could, Grace came up behind me and said, "I hear you paid Rudolph back."

I turned to her, drew a breath. "No," I said. "Not true. I wish I had." Before I left St. Pete that summer, I stopped by the theater and gave Rudolph my bankroll—three hundred fifty dollars, the sum of my unspent stolen money. "I'm sorry," I said again.

Rudolph shook his head. "I have insurance," he said. "I'm covered." He was on his hands and knees in the lobby, pulling up the carpet.

"Keep it," I said. "It's yours."

He nodded then. "Where'd you get it?" he said.

"I sold my car," I said, using the answer I had made up that morning while packing.

"You didn't have to do that," Rudolph said, holding the money out to me. "Really, I'm covered."

I didn't take it. When I left, I hitchhiked into downtown St. Pete, where my car was stashed in an hourly parking lot, then drove north to school.

It didn't surprise me that Grace knew about the money. Rudolph had told her. She got the story wrong because he had lied and told her I'd paid for everything. I straightened her out.

"I never minded you watching me in the window," she told me later that evening. "I liked it. The window was dark. I could only see your face every once in a while. You looked like a ghost. First time it scared me, but then I was glad you finally saw me that way. Then I knew you wouldn't be jealous of Rudolph anymore."

I've never been sure how Grace knew that last bit or why it was so true. We began to see each other again that summer and I saw her naked many times during those months. Years later, after we were married, I even saw Rudolph's painting of Grace, when we went to visit him at his home in Pensacola. By then all the confessions had been made.

It's notable that upon my return to Gainesville, after the summer in St. Pete, I found that I was not entirely unpopular with the brothers in the fraternity that had blackballed me. I saw them all the time around campus, in classes, in bars, at various parties. Once I started talking to them, they were friendly. They regretted what had happened, they told me. Occasionally one of them would clap a hand on my shoulder and say how sorry he was about the whole thing.

After a while I just told them to forget it, that it had been like a trial, that I was better for it. The silly thing was, I believed what I said.

Grace
Speaks

G race never fussed over decisions, only made them and moved on. For her, life was not a garden; there was no need to dwell, kneel, or tend.

It was generally agreed that she didn't think ahead. Grace herself liked to admit that she had no conception of the future. "You need to visualize yourself," a friend told her once on an escalator. "If you really see something happening, it will." But since Grace had no real interest in the future, the visualizing didn't work. "I just see me," she told her friend. "Me, just like I am."

She forgot things—leaving bills unpaid, letters unopened, thank-you notes unaddressed, for months at a time. All around her apartment there were cocktail glasses spread so randomly, notched and tipped in so many tight places, that it looked as if someone had thrown them at the room like a handful of thimbles. Once she left a toaster on her coffee table for two months straight through two parties and a visit from her mother's family. "Jesus, Gracie," her Uncle

Alfred said when he sat down, waving his cigarette at the toaster, "I'll take two slices of rye."

When she left Florida for New York, her parents thought she had made the decision too quickly. "This is like over-night," her mother said when Grace told her, and she was right. Though her friends had been urging her to move north with them for months, Grace had only made the decision the night before, in bed with the moon cutting in through the window. She had decided by rolling over. She said to herself, When I roll over this time I'll have a decision. Though this worked convincingly for her, she knew she would have a hard time drawing up explanations for her mother. "I can go there," she said, when the subject came up. "I have a place to stay."

Before she left, she took her parents to dinner at a Hun-garian restaurant that she liked. Her father drank glass after glass of the woody table wine. At one point she looked at him for a long moment and he snapped, "What do you want? You want me to get red-rimmed and teary?" But Grace had only been wondering how she would wrestle the check from him when the time came.

In New York, she got a job mixing dyes for a textile de-signer. It was precision work. She was forced to recognize tiny things, things she hadn't noticed before. One beaker might draw a larger drop of dye than another. Window light could corrupt an afternoon's work. Flush with her new job, concentration came easily and Grace grew to love her table full of bottles and tubes and petri dishes.

At night she scrubbed the dye from her fingernails and made tiny sandwiches. Along with her best friend from work, she developed a taste for scotch, which they ordered first, before water even, when they went out together. Then she drank too much at an Easter party in Brooklyn and spent the next week with the taste of ham in her throat.

"You live an unconsidered life," her mother told her not long after that. "No time for church, no time for decent thinking."

"Decent thinking?" Grace said. They were on the phone. Grace was sipping water, fighting the urge to chew ice.

"Reasoning," her mother said. "Questioning."

"I do that," Grace said, holding the water up to the sunlight, looking for sediment, insects, whatever was there.

"Your father says you can't reason, that you don't know how."

"I'm okay," Grace said.

Her mother sighed. "You see? I said you can't reason. You said, 'I'm okay.' That doesn't follow."

Grace was silent then, unsure of what her mother wanted next. "Nothing connects," her mother went on. "Honey, things have to connect."

Months later, Grace began seeing a sportswriter. He brought her his articles to read, features on alcoholic point guards, sidebars on women's softball teams. He liked to present them to her in the kitchen and then leave her to read them amongst the onions she was chopping. At first she read them closely, trying hard to remember the rules of basketball, ignoring the statistics, inching forward for the turn of a phrase. She worried that she could only come up with a few words of response on each, but the sportswriter seemed to love it when she handed him the manuscript and said something terse like "sad" or "tight."

He loved leading her by the hand through the recesses
and tunnels of Madison Square Garden, up the spiral stair-
case to the press box at Shea. On the streets he always took
the lead, pulling her forward to the next corner. He gave
her silent hand signals as they walked, squeezes that sometimes bore down so tight that she could feel his college ring
like a tiny bullet in her palm. She never complained, and
although she knew the hand pulses to be his traffic signals—
stop, go, turn here, stay close—she never heeded him much
or squeezed his hand back. She sensed that all of his leading
would have bothered her once, but she began to admire his
sense of direction and took his speed to be a sign of quick
thinking, the kind her mother might admire. She came to
love lagging near the end of his reach.

When he kissed her, the sportswriter was too rough and
all Grace gave him was teeth until she felt him easing up a
little. She liked the way he hooked his arm around her back
and lifted her slightly, no matter what position they were in.
She didn't take this as leading so much as rising, and she
arched her back so that he would do it again and again.

The sportswriter said he loved her broad knowledge of
movies. In college she had worked in a movie house and had
watched every offering for free, some of them many times
over. She found it easy to call up casting questions and plot
twists. The sportswriter loved it. When she came up with an
answer for a gathering of friends—"Natalie Wood," say—
he would smile and tap his finger to his temple admiringly.
That did annoy her, so she began throwing out wrong answers until he quit asking in public. Still he liked to draw
comparisons between her knowledge of movies and his own
memory for sports trivia, suggesting that the two somehow
complemented each other.

★   ★   ★

One snowy night in March, with the sportswriter out of town at a basketball tournament, Grace went to a party across the street from her apartment. The hostess, Grace's friend from college, told everyone as they entered, "This is a party all about junk food." That puzzled Grace, but she gave up her coat and watched the crowd get happier and happier as the platters of hamburgers and french fries kept coming. There were packets of ketchup and relish on every flat surface. One woman brought a baby, who toddled around a coffee table with a tampon in one hand. The crowd seemed to love it. But after a minute, a man knelt down and gently took the tampon from the baby's hand. He shook his head disdainfully at those who scolded him. "I don't like that," he said. To the baby, who started crying as he tucked the tampon away on top of a bookshelf, he whispered, "There, there, bubba."

Surprisingly Grace recognized him as Dan Foley, someone she had worked with at the movie house in St. Pete, someone who liked to shave money from the snack bar. A thief. He was a vandal too. They were mutual friends of the hostess's. Grace had even kissed him several times.

He approached her later, with two clinking glasses of whiskey pinched between his fingers. "The thief," Grace said.

He handed her a glass and smiled. "I paid everything back."

"So I heard." But Grace had heard nothing. She was giving him the benefit of the doubt.

Foley was now an architect. "I iron my own shirts," he said. "I only have seven."

When he visited her the next day at her office, she was glad to see him. Foley sat straight down at her desk and fingered the bottles of dye, asking countless questions about primary colors and fabrics. She found that she didn't mind explaining these simple processes, as he seemed genuinely curious. Each step illuminated the next. "My father is an undertaker," Foley said, passing his hand over the desk. "This reminds me of the way he works."

"What do you mean by that?" Grace asked.

"He understands the job completely," he said. "He knows how to control things step by step. Like cause and effect. He's always starting one thing and then another and none of it seems to be going anywhere."

"Does it?" Grace asked.

"It comes together sort of suddenly, just at the end," Foley said. "Then you can see why he started every little thing, how he was moving, thinking ahead. It's really a job." He paused and looked at her equipment. "But you know it's also all these neat little jars, all these instruments. They remind me of the embalming room."

Grace stared at him. "No insult intended," Foley said. Then he spun in the chair, pointed at some samples on the windowsill and started in with the questions again.

Foley was small-boned. He had been lifting weights since college and Grace liked the way his new muscles troubled him. She found that he was light, and that night as they were kissing she tried to lift him and found not only that she could, but that he liked it.

They ate lunch together quite often in the coming weeks. He told her about his job, about old cars he had bought and sold, about his father's business, whatever seemed to be on his mind, and Grace never wanted him to stop. Each story progressed toward the next, until she found that he could tell stories about the two of them—their walks, their tics, the way both of them snatched at the check every time. She realized that he had reached the present with his stories, without her noticing, not until that very moment.

She continued seeing the sportswriter. He had long ago asked her to marry him. Clearly it was still heady to him that she hadn't given him an answer. He wrote things for her—including a sort of master plan of their future. He meant this to comfort her and it worked to some degree. She enjoyed reading his scrawled letters, filled with savings schedules, economic forecasts, houses, then new houses, and finally the children one by one. It was like reading fiction. "How do you know these things?" she once asked him. "How can you see them so clearly?" But the sportswriter laughed. "Those aren't really facts," he said. "That's not knowledge."

Often, she would sit up at night, drawing and redrawing each of the men in her mind's eye. It was as close to a vision as she could muster. She could see them, stark as photographs, feel them as heavy and tangible as overcoats. The sportswriter, cocked and ready, at the doorway. The thief, slight and tense, slinking down on top of her.

When she was in high school, Grace's father kept her from driving until she was eighteen. Even then he would only let her drive to the grocery store. "You watch your eggs," he would say, handing her the keys. "Promise me you'll put them on the floor in the back seat."

Life was a series of promises to her father in those days. She promised to get a degree in education. Not to smoke. To drive the back streets, not Gulf Boulevard. To lock the doors of the car, of the house. To check the depth of the water before diving. To stay away from Cubans.

It seemed a patchwork collection of worries to her. She could see that her father was afraid, more than anything else, but she could never see where the next line would be drawn. Later, in New York, she realized that men never explained why they drew lines, why they asked promises. So as she became even more circumscribed—keeping the sportswriter at bay, giving the thief only her work number—she felt that she was no longer working from instinct. She had drawn lines, real ones, so that they could balance one another. She gave each one a separate life—day and night, work and home, sports and stock market. Foley told her stories of his childhood, of his weekends, told her jokes, drew cartoons on the placemats of the diners where they ate. The sportswriter gave her books, introduced her to editors, publishers, and Hall of Fame third basemen.

At first they were distinct, but soon they merged into one presence in her mind and for a while she was genuinely careless—mistaking one for the other, missing dates, leaving calls unanswered. When they finally became aware of one another, it was the thief, with his sweet stories and his manic curiosity, who left her. The sportswriter took this as a sort of victory and there she was again, reaching for explanations, struggling to make the promises he so wanted to hear.

After Grace agreed to marry the sportswriter, she immediately began to have doubts. When she told them to her mother, her mother did not want to hear. "You have to move forward on faith," she said.

"Why?" Grace said.

"You've made a promise here," her mother said. "It's a clear road. Move forward."

Her friends were astonished that she had given in to the sportswriter. Few of them liked him. Once, over a bowl of pepper soup, a friend asked her openly, "Why?" and Grace pushed the conversation past the question, without answering. Her friend pursued. "It's good that he's tall, I guess, and he can write. But why now?" For that, and for the questions that followed, Grace had no answers, though when she found herself lying or begging off, it seemed a step forward. So she kept on until she could see nothing else except that next lie, the next evasion. For a time, all of this made her blind with faith.

One night the sportswriter showed up at her door after a Knicks game, very drunk. Grace let him in without turning on the lights. He slumped on the couch. He'd had, he claimed, a series of reversals. No one liked his novel. He'd been missing deadlines. There were gambling losses.

At first Grace sat on the coffee table and commiserated. Would he lose his job, she asked. He snapped to then and said, "Is that what you're worried about?" She held his hand. But the sportswriter wasn't listening to her; he pulled his hand from hers more than once, whirled from her as much as the couch would allow. Soon Grace just let him talk.

"Where do I go from here?" he said at one point, his head back, eyes closed. Grace could see that he was edging toward passing out. Then he flung himself full out on the couch. Before he fell asleep he pulled a glass out from one of the cracks and dropped it on the carpet. "Glasses," he said. "Jesus."

When he was fully asleep, Grace got up and turned on the lights. Her apartment suddenly seemed like a sickroom, too colorless, too painfully bright. She flicked off the lights again, threw a blanket over the sportswriter and went to the window.

Grace could see directly down into the apartments across the street. She often looked in on her friend's place, the one who threw the junk food party. Tonight her friend was having yet another dinner party, and Grace could see that the table was full of plates and wine bottles and that every chair was full. The guests were turned toward someone at the end of the table, someone telling a joke or a story, leaning forward, drawing them in with his hands, pausing every once in a while for a swallow of wine. Soon she could see that it was Foley.

She watched the party for an hour, half sitting on her radiator, squinting to make out the players, but she could only be sure of the thief. As the volleys of conversation seemed to bounce his way again and again, she recognized his gestures—the way he pointed and jabbed in the air as he told a joke, the way he shook his head slowly as he cracked a smile, the way he laughed riotously at his friends' stories.

Soon she began to feel that she was sitting with him, next to him—the glasses half full, the cigarette smoke hanging low. His weight was on the table, on his elbows. Someone, in another room, was putting on a record album. Then he reached for her, with something new—a question—or something familiar—a stalk of celery—and then she was back on the radiator.

So when she turned away from the window, it was much like the time she had rolled over in bed to make a decision; it was done. The blue city light fell through the window in wedges, from above, as if it had weight. When she shook the sportswriter awake, she felt sorry for him as he tried to gain his bearings.

"I have something to tell you," she said, but he rolled over and murmured, "Later. In the morning."

"No," she said. "Wake up."

Finally he sat up and angrily rubbed his eyes. "I'm waiting," he said. He held a hand up in the air and shook it like a tambourine. "Silence all. Grace speaks."

She almost laughed at his attempt to affect ceremony.

It seemed appropriate. When she looked away for a moment, he threw his hands up and snapped, "Well?"

How would she begin to tell him of the vision she'd had? She might lean forward and start in, speaking thoughtfully, choosing her words carefully. It was the future, she could say. She could see it. No telling why.

Foley's
Luck

There were times when Foley felt himself cursed by a small mistake. Trouble would follow. He tried to live with his bad luck, to wait it out, but bad things just piled up and up until he found himself cataloguing his life, figuring to himself, How did I start this? Where did this begin?

One July night he hit a fox with his Chevrolet and a particular string of bad luck followed. It happened outside Sarasota, on a little farm road that he liked to use as a short-cut home. He was with Grace, his wife, who yelped when the fox slid beneath their headlights. Foley felt the fox hit in the bones of his feet. He pulled the car to a stop on the shoulder and looked back. Grace put her hands over her face. She was pregnant, nearly six months, and she rested her elbows on the slope of her belly, cradling her head in her palms. It was a gesture Foley had seen a lot of lately. Sometimes he woke up late at night and found her like this.

"That was too much," she said.

"It was a fox," Foley stated. Behind them, in the light

thrown from a distant barn, he could see the silhouette of the animal as it lifted itself again and again. "Oh, Jesus," he said.

Grace kept her hands on her face. "It's still alive, isn't it?"

Foley put the car in reverse. "It's still alive," he said. "Yes."

But when they got to the fox it lay flat on the side of the road, not moving. Foley got out and checked. The fox had a bloody mouth. It was dead. He told Grace, who had stayed in the car, with the windows rolled up.

"Are you sure?" she said. From behind the windshield, her voice came to him with the same metallic ring it had when they yelled to each other underwater. They loved doing that. Years earlier, at the NYU natatorium, he had proposed to her underwater. She surprised him by coming up from the deep end knowing full well what he had said.

He got back in behind the wheel, and Grace repeated her question. "Are you sure it's dead?"

"Dead is dead. I know dead."

Though he tried not to think about it, the event pained him the rest of the way home for a number of reasons. He had seen, if only in shadow, the fox's death spasms; it was a young fox, very small, and there had been so little blood. When they pulled away, Grace shot a glance out the side window. "Looks like it's sleeping." Foley ignored her and drove off. But after Grace said that, he wished that he had touched the fox to make sure that it was dead. Even as he pulled in the driveway, he considered turning back to check, but didn't, allowing what he figured to be good sense to prevail.

The next morning Foley's bad luck started in earnest. As he was walking down the street to buy a newspaper, he noticed a rosebush in front of a house four doors from his. The roses were past full bloom, spread so wide and fat that he almost didn't recognize them as roses. He reached down to smell one, taking the stem of the flower between two fingers. But as his nose touched the petals, the flower fell apart in his hand. He hadn't expected that and when he pulled back in surprise, the bush snagged his sleeve and shook, so that the other flowers fell apart too.

He stood over the ruined rosebush for a moment, then turned and walked on. It was early morning, likely too early for anyone to have seen this happen. But he worried more about how things fell apart when he touched them, quickly and reliably, like some chemical reaction.

Things got worse. There were no newspapers at the gas station, nor at the grocery store a mile farther down. When he arrived home, thirty minutes later than usual, Grace was still in bed. "My back hurts," she said, without rising. "Where were you?"

When he touched her arm, he felt that she was burning up with fever. He called the doctor, who told him to bring her in to his office right away. He sat Grace up and helped her dress. "Should I be scared?" she asked him. "Should I worry about the baby?" Hushing her, he told her no, not to worry, then buttoned her blouse. The doctor had sounded alarmed, though. Only when he had her waiting on the couch in the living room did Foley return to the bedroom to pack for the hospital.

At noon Grace was admitted to the hospital with what the doctor termed a major kidney infection. They tried to be calm while the doctor talked with them about the possibilities of the infection shifting to the uterus, about antibiotics and fluids, the chances of premature labor. He illustrated every point of anatomy with a mechanical pencil borrowed from Foley, tracing in the air the curving fallopian tubes, the sloping ureters, then jabbing in the area of the infection. When the doctor left, he took Foley's pencil. Grace was falling off to sleep. "Him and that pencil," she said. "It was making me sick."

Grace slept fitfully for two days. Her fever fell, then disappeared. Soon the doctor told them that the danger was over. Grace was to stay another week in the hospital, he said, then have another week of bed rest at home. Foley, who had spent two nights in the hospital waiting room, made plans for her return. "You'll need water," the doctor said. "Lots of water." He was talking about water to drink, of course, but for Foley, who left the house in a rush and had not yet returned, this brought momentary visions of fire. He hurried home.

When he turned in the driveway, the garage door was open. Nothing seemed to be missing or out of place, but the door from the garage to the kitchen was also open. This alarmed him. When he walked in the house Foley found a large black dog standing in the center of his dining room table eating the last of some angel food cake off a small plate.

The dog lifted its head and growled. Foley took a step forward and shouted, "Oh, come on! Off the table! Get out of here!" The dog flinched and growled louder. Then Foley noticed the streams and ribbons of trash all over the carpet in the dining room. He grew furious. He pointed a finger at the door and shouted at the dog. "Out!" he said and the dog barked, scrambled forward, scratching the hardwood tabletop, then leapt at him.

Foley found himself moving without a thought. He bent one knee, turned back toward the kitchen and tried to jump for the nearest counter, but the dog's bite caught him in midleap. He thumped to the floor and the dog thrashed, pulling at his calf. Foley screamed, kicked with his other leg. For a moment the dog let go, before biting down again, this time higher up, near the knee.

While the dog locked down tighter on his leg, Foley found that he could hear two things: the clicking of the dog's nails against the linoleum and the tearing of his trousers as it pulled him back on his belly again and again. This gave him the strange sensation that he was hardly a part of this. Even as he kicked and swore and spit, he found that he had to remind himself, This is happening to me. I'm in the middle of this.

Soon he began playing dead and the dog stopped thrashing, though it stayed locked. Foley lay still, his head facing away from the dog, and kept one eye on the second hand of his watch. "It didn't hurt," he would tell friends later. "I was just afraid it might never end."

After four minutes, forty seconds the dog let go. Foley checked himself from taking a breath, from moving even the slightest bit. Fifty-eight seconds later the dog walked far enough away for him to jump to his feet and up onto the kitchen counter. The dog snarled, but did not come at him this time. Foley reached into the dirty dishes in the sink, pulled out a steak knife and threw it at the dog. He missed, then reached back and threw a jar of sugar, which caught the dog flush in the side. Then a can of V-8. Then a bigger knife. Then a potted plant from the shelf above the sink. The dog leapt back and forth around these things, until suddenly it ran straight out the door.

Foley didn't look at his leg. He could see that it was bad enough from the blood that covered his kitchen floor. Finally he got down, shut the door, and called Quinn, his neighbor, who came over right away. As Quinn wrapped his leg, Foley felt himself grow dizzy. "Is it bad?" he asked. "It feels pretty bad."

But Quinn shook his head, kept his eyes on the job. As he was helping Foley stand, he looked into the kitchen, at the bloody floor. "Looks something like a butcher shop," he said.

"Bloodletting," Foley said, laughing despite himself. "Human sacrifice."

Suddenly, or so it seemed to Foley, they were at the hospital. Quinn stood at the admitting desk talking to a woman with a blue clipboard. Foley was flat on his back on a gurney a few feet away, reading their lips. He could only hear the soft canned music and someone nearby folding paper, stuffing envelopes.

The woman at the desk: "Insurance?"

Then Quinn, shrugging: "I don't know. We share lawn tools."

Foley's story made the paper and while he was in the hospital, with his leg stitched and elevated, someone broke into his house and stole his television and his coin collection.

At the doctor's request, he sent Quinn out looking for the dog, giving him detailed descriptions, sketches even. Quinn did his best, posting bills on telephone poles, in gas stations and junkyards, but nothing came of it. The morning paper ran a follow-up story, with another warning about the dog. It did no good. After forty-eight hours the doctors recommended rabies shots. Before the first shot, his doctor tapped out the air bubbles from the syringe and said, "You're lucky. You'll only have one a week for a month. Used to be one a day for a month." The injections were made into Foley's stomach. He vomited furiously for hours afterward.

Quinn was the first to call it bad luck, and he recommended throwing the I Ching. "It works for my family," he said.

"My wife won't even go to the store without throwing those little coins."

But Foley formulated his own plan to bring his life back onto its former plane. Taking several weeks off from work to recover and take care of Grace, he decided to learn to garden, bought several books to that effect. This would bring him closer to the earth, he figured, give him a chance to focus. He bought a tray of pachysandra, a large bag of mulch, some fertilizer and a gardening kit, but as he knelt for the first time the stitches in the back of his leg popped. Grace had to leave her sickbed to drive him back to the hospital. "Learn to take care of yourself," she said as they drove. "Try something you can do sitting down. Like chess."

"Bonsai trees," Foley said. "Jigsaw puzzles." He meant to mock her, but she was enthusiastic about his ideas.

"Yes! Try barbecuing, maybe," Grace said, stopping at a red light. "Do a hooked rug!"

Foley had a dish towel tied around his leg. He decided that he had been fighting the world. Of Grace's suggestions he liked barbecuing the best. On the way home from the hospital, with his leg newly wrapped and restitched, despite Grace's objections, they stopped at a warehouse outlet store. Foley limped up to a forklift.

"I want a grill," he said to the salesclerk, who looked down from the driver's seat sipping a diet soda. "A big one."

"You want a grill?" the salesclerk said. His hair was dirty, mashed down under a plastic hard hat. He squinted one eye at Foley when he talked, as if he couldn't believe what he was hearing.

Foley nodded.

"I think you want a smoker," the clerk said, holding up a single finger. "I don't think a grill will do you right."

"I want to barbecue," Foley said. Grace was waiting in the car. His leg throbbed. He wanted out.

The clerk leaned down. "Everything's better in a

smoker. Chicken, duck. It's so tender, it just falls apart." He illustrated his point by balling up his left hand like a small animal, pinching as if to check for doneness.

Foley waved him on. He was in no mood to fight. "Get me a smoker, then."

The clerk put the forklift in reverse. A beeper started up. "You'll be happy," he said. "It's man's greatest invention."

Foley bought the smoker without opening the box, without realizing that he would have to assemble it. Its cylindrical shape surprised him as he put it together on his dining room table. There were other surprises too. The smoking process itself was alien to him. According to the enclosed pamphlet—"Smoking with Pleasure"—it would take an entire afternoon to smoke a chicken. Foley couldn't imagine what to do in the interim. The pamphlet suggested a movie.

He lit the fire in the early morning, set the meats on at noon and spent the afternoon sitting next to the smoker, contemplating the temperature gauge, which had three readings: Warm, Ideal, and Hot. He smoked pork chops the first night, then ribs, and then chicken. At the pamphlet's suggestion, he experimented with different brands of charcoal in an attempt to better control temperature and added different woods for flavoring, mesquite and hickory to begin with, but later more exotic hardwoods like cherry and apple. He learned to smoke cheeses, hard-boiled eggs, corn and zucchini and not to peek under the lid of the smoker, as this released too much heat and moisture.

Sometimes he left for an hour or two, as when he went for his rabies shots or to pick up Grace's prescriptions. It gave him great pleasure when he returned to find that all was well with the smoker, that the needle was rock solid steady between Ideal and Hot.

Neither of them tired of the smoked offerings. For her

part, Grace craved Foley's apple-smoked apple slices and never turned her nose up at any of his attempts. She recovered slowly and Foley, inspired by the timing and pace of the smoker, was patient. He took an extra week from work, even after Grace was clearly up and around. His stitches had long since been pulled.

On the day before he returned to work he smoked a beef brisket. They had invited the Quinns for dinner and at midafternoon Lee, the Quinns' nine-year-old, led a pack of bicycling friends into Foley's back yard.

"What are we having tonight?" Lee said. All around him, his friends made revving noises. Motorcycles.

"Brisket," Foley said. "Maybe corn too. Do you want corn?"

"What is that thing?" Lee said, pointing to the smoker.

"It's a smoker," Foley said. Lee stared dully at the smoker as Foley began explaining its innards. But the boys grew restless, began peeling away. Lee was the last to turn. Foley yelled after him, "The smoker is man's greatest invention." He echoed the salesclerk gladly, gratefully.

That night the brisket was a great success, and Foley, giddy with the sense that he had reversed his bad luck, told the Quinns the whole story of hitting the fox and the bad luck that had followed—the roses, the sold-out newspaper, Grace's illness, the dog, the break-in, the shots, the gardening, and the burst stitches. He had told the story in bits and pieces over the past weeks, to everyone who would listen. People tended to commiserate, first shaking their heads. "Some luck," "bad luck," then nodding their heads yes, they understood.

Now Quinn and his wife, Maggie, sat with a hurricane candle burning between their plates. Maggie set down her corncob as Foley finished the story with the smoker, suggesting that it had turned his luck. "It really did the trick," he said, taking a long sip of wine.

"You say a fox started all of this?" Maggie said, picking up a slice of brisket between her thumb and forefinger. She bit down on the meat and pulled at it.

Foley nodded and stood up. Lee was at the corner of the house with a flashlight, looking for lizards under the air-conditioning unit. Foley could see only his sneakers. "Watermelon, Lee! Do you want watermelon?"

Lee shouted something that none of them could hear, and Foley went inside to get the watermelon and a long knife. He took Grace's plate with him. When he got to the kitchen he could hear Maggie through the window. "True, true. Very true," she said.

When he came back out with the melon, Maggie leaned back in her chair and stared at him. He cut five thick wedges and passed them out. "Which way was it running?" Maggie said, when he finally sat down again.

"What?" Foley said.

"Which way was the fox running?"

"Across the road, Maggie," Grace piped in. Quinn snorted into a bite of his melon.

Maggie waved them off and looked at Foley. "Which way?"

"I don't know exactly," Foley said. "West to east, I guess. Roughly."

"Left to right?" Maggie said, taking a large bite of melon. Foley noticed that she had lopped off a good hunk of rind with it.

"I guess so," he said.

At that Maggie banged the table with the palm of her hand. Foley looked at Grace in puzzlement. They hardly knew the Quinns. He liked Quinn, though he often seemed moody and he had begun taking Foley's tools without asking. Maggie was Grace's friend more than his. During Grace's recovery, Maggie brought poultices in the mornings and various teas in the afternoons. She often rubbed Grace's neck. For Foley's wounds, she only suggested ice.

Maggie set her watermelon down ceremoniously. "In Eastern Europe, the fox is a mischief animal," she said. "So what you're saying really makes sense."

"How so?" Foley said.

"When a mischief animal appears on the left, forget it."

"Forget what?" Quinn said.

"Just forget it is all," Maggie said. "You're in for trouble."

Grace nodded. Lee called to his mother from behind the house. Again Foley couldn't hear what he said. Maggie stood. "You did the right thing," she said to him. "You centered yourself. You killed off the bad luck."

Foley wanted to believe that. When the Quinns left, with Lee holding their empty casserole over his head with both hands, like some Indian woman bearing water from a well, Foley waved, and congratulated himself on his instinct. "I was really falling in a hole," he told Grace as they rinsed the plates. "Somehow I knew how to stop myself."

The next day Foley realized that when he had said that, about falling in a hole, Grace had only shrugged her shoulders and kept working. He let the subject die. In the weeks that followed he told the story less often. He began to sense that it was getting old. His co-workers made excuses to wander when he did start in. He tried to let the string of bad luck fade from his memory.

Months later he found a thick book called *The History of Luck* at a bookstore in downtown Tampa. It seemed a good gift for Maggie, to whom he still felt somehow indebted. He bought and read it quickly, finding nothing whatsoever about Eastern Europe or mischief animals. One chapter focused on a people who believed that luck had to be maintained. The author compared their conception of luck to an automobile in need of constant tuning. These people chanted all day, to keep their luck going. "They devote every breath to luck," the author wrote. The chants were simple, the book said, so that children could begin them at an early age. There was a list of typical chants like "We are small creatures" and "We are tossed by the wind." The chants brought to mind the tornadoes he'd heard about as a boy, the ones that lifted a cow from its pasture and deposited it miles away, apparently no worse for the wear, on the median of the interstate. Cows like that never gave milk again.

The book had one short, self-help appendix, in which the author suggested that bad luck should be charted. "Writing things down," he suggested, "allows the unlucky person a visual thread to which, logically, there must then be a clear and perceptible end."

So Foley took to stringing out the events for his own benefit, at his desk on a legal pad or in a coffee shop on the curling edge of a placemat. Whenever he wrote out the series, connecting each event to the next with a neat architectural arrow, he found that there were incidents of bad luck that he had not yet thought to add to the list: His mother breaking her foot on the morning Grace went into the hospital. A bounced check that arrived while he was at the hospital. The keloid scar that left his calf looking mangled long after things had healed. At first he wrote these things below the original string like footnotes. When he told the story with these new details, people perceived them as fabrications. No one wanted to hear them. "Every time you tell that story you add something new," a friend told him once at lunch in a steamy courtyard restaurant. "It's beginning to sound like bullshit."

Foley knew then that he could never tell it again. And he didn't, but he kept writing out the string every week or two, now freely adding in any new details that occurred to him. The list changed slightly in each version, except that it always began with the fox and ended with the smoker.

Though he told himself the list was only a diversion, he strove for accuracy of detail. He began to see the whole thing as some forgotten formula equation, waiting to be reconstructed for the benefit of the ages; he would be the scientist, the historian, the neutral observer.

His daughter Sophie was born in the fall and he hardly considered it bad luck that she was slightly jaundiced. The doctor recommended sunlight. "Sit her in the sun for a while," he said. "Sometimes you have to jump-start the liver."

Foley did this gladly, sitting in the back yard next to the cradle in the early morning, when the sun would not burn Sophie. Grace appreciated it too, as she could sleep late or lie in bed and read. Gradually Sophie grew less yellow, but Foley kept up the routine until the weather got too cold.

One afternoon some months later, he came home early from work and found that the sun was out. It was plenty warm, but not brutally hot, so he loosened his tie, picked up Sophie and carried her out to sit with him in the sun. It had been a wet winter. The grass was longer and greener than usual. He spread a blanket and put Sophie down in her infant seat. He then stretched out next to her.

When Sophie fell asleep, he tried to doze, but the Quinns were having an argument next door. Things were loud. Foley heard shouting, then thumping and door-slamming. As he dropped off he found himself considering the structure of their house. How could it be that he could hear into their lives so clearly?

Foley snapped awake when Quinn kicked open the screen door. Foley sat up and saw Quinn walking determinedly across his lawn toward him. His first thought was that Quinn was leaving, running out. He stood to call to Quinn, to stop him and offer counsel.

Quinn came right at Foley and pointed a finger. "A nine-year-old boy!"

They must be having trouble with Lee, Foley figured. He looked down at Sophie, who was beginning to stir. He decided he could spare a moment to talk with Quinn, who seemed to be coming over for a gripe session. Sliding his hands into his pockets, Foley started forward. "What did he do?"

Quinn walked straight up to him, still shouting. "What do you think he did? They were all doing it!" He came up to within inches of Foley's face. Foley put a hand on Quinn's chest, but Quinn slapped it away. Foley could see Maggie then, standing behind the screen door, calling to her husband. Lee was at her side.

"Take it easy!" Foley said, taking a step back and a step away from Sophie, who was now crying. "Doing what? What are you talking about?"

"Smoking cigarettes!" Quinn shouted, jabbing Foley in the chest. "You told him smoking was the greatest thing in the world!" He jabbed again.

Foley put his hands up, palms out, like a traffic cop. "Stop! I never said that!"

Quinn turned and called to Lee. "Isn't that right, Lee?" he said, pointing a finger at Foley. "Didn't he tell you that?"

"Wait a minute!" Foley said. He could see Lee nodding.

"Lee! Maggie!" He made a move toward them, but Quinn spun around and gave him a big two-handed shove. Foley stumbled. "What is this?" he said. "What's going on here?" Quinn took two running steps toward him and hit him with a forearm in the chin.

Foley flew backward. His feet went out from under him. He felt one hand touch the gravel at the side of his house; then his head hit hard against the foundation, and he was knocked out. Later he remembered a momentary worry that he had hit the hose spout, that it had buried itself in his head somehow. He remembered that, and Sophie's crying.

He woke in the hospital, at the entrance to the emergency room, on an ambulance gurney. When he tried to sit up a voice said, "He's awake!" Then a hand pushed him back down flat. Although he couldn't see her, he knew that Grace was there too, because he could hear that Sophie was nearby, still crying. He tried to be still.

He spent a week in the hospital, with warnings about head and neck injuries read off to him regularly by nurses and doctors. A police officer visited him on the third day and asked if he wanted to press charges against Quinn. Foley said no, that it was a misunderstanding. It had taken him a day or two to figure that Lee had misinterpreted his remark about the smoker, the salesclerk's line about mankind's greatest invention. He told Grace, who told Quinn.

"He cried," she said the next day. "I was so mad I could have spit."

Foley began his charting again: Fox → Rose → Newspaper → Kidney → and so on. When he got to smoker, the usual end of the list, he hesitated, then penciled in Jaundice and then Fight. He quickly wrote out the list again. Then again. It now had no natural end.

⋆   ⋆   ⋆

The story might go on and on from there, Foley knew—
him spinning out his endless string of bad luck. Or he might
try to break that luck again. He tried using the chants he
had read about, but the repetition was hard to maintain. The
book had recommended personal rituals: one cream, one
sugar; buttering his toast; warm-ups before running. He remembered that baseball players often touched the catcher's
head before leaving the dugout. He brushed Sophie's head
with his fingers every morning before leaving for the office.
Grace made him stop. "You'll only end up blaming her,"
she said.

The fight did not prove to be a natural end to the list,
in fact. Instead, the list got longer. Foley kept up the charting in a spiral notebook, a page for each entry, first week
by week, then day by day. Flat tires. Sprained ankles. Early
frosts. Audits. Thrown rods. Paper cuts. Spilled coffee. Bad
movies. Leg cramps. Basement flooding. Poor timing.

After close to a year of this, Grace took over by hiding
the notebook away. She treated him like an addict. "One
day," she said, half teasing. "Just go one day without it."
She returned the book the next day, then took it away again,
repeating the cycle over and over. One evening while chopping scallions she told him that she had thrown it out. It
didn't bother him.

"Good," Foley said. "Maybe that will change my luck."
He went to the refrigerator and pulled out a beer.

"You act like your luck is all bad," Grace said. There
was a forlorn tone to her voice. She had long since given up
getting angry on the subject of luck. "You have a beautiful
daughter and you just got a raise. What kind of luck is
that?"

It was true. He had gotten a raise. Another soon followed. They were able to trade up on the Chevrolet and redesign the kitchen. Sophie learned to walk on the day after the new carpeting was installed in the living room. They painted the house, screened in the porch, installed a handsome patio and hired a landscaper.

One Christmas Grace brought out a large ungainly box with a blue ribbon tied around it. She laughed and set it in his lap. "This is a healing gesture," she said, as Sophie clapped. The puppy scrambling around the inside of the box grew to be his constant companion, his loyal defender.

"Remember your bad luck?" Grace asked him years later, on the afternoon they learned she was pregnant again. Foley, recently promoted, shook his head and lifted his wineglass. "Ancient history."

But he did remember. There were days when things came clearly, and he could recite the list from memory. He considered the string of bad luck to still be there, only hidden now, hanging over him like some jungle net drawn taut by his occasional recitation of the list. He even added incidents from time to time. It was now a matter of control, he figured.

Each time he started in on the list, he called up the incident with the fox, the feel of its bones as his old car rumbled over it. Once, as he was driving the old farm road from Sarasota, he stopped at the place where he remembered hitting the fox. He did some kicking about in the dry grass there, with no real hope of finding anything. Then he climbed back in the car and sat. That was the trigger, he told himself. The change started here. "Fox," he said as he turned the key. He went on, one word at a time.

*   *   *

Soon after his son Nick was born they sold the house. They found an older place on a lot by the Gulf, out in Madeira Beach. On the day before the movers came, they had one last party for their neighborhood friends.

Foley hauled the smoker up from the basement and threw a rack of ribs on in the morning. He added two chickens at noon and vegetables throughout the afternoon. He smoked on a mixture of beer-soaked mesquite and cider-soaked apple wood. It was his own development.

That evening several families arrived all at once and the house, with the boxes pushed in the corners and the furniture askew, seemed jolly and full of life. Foley passed out cocktails, while Sophie toddled around with a plastic tray of celery and cream cheese. Grace put on music—fiddles and accordions. To Foley, it brought weddings to mind.

As he stepped out to get the ribs off the smoker, he bumped into Maggie Quinn, who was on her way inside with an ashtray in one hand and a drink in the other. Foley and Grace had resumed a tenuous friendship with the Quinns. Quinn had sought counseling for his temper and with time Foley figured that was enough. Maggie blocked the bottom step from the new porch, so Foley moved to one side. "Well," she said, looking up at him. "Are you going to kiss me?"

There were several children lingering on the patio, near the smoker. None of them had heard. Foley ignored the pass. He liked the evening too much. The milling of bodies, the occasional dance step, the flicker of cigarettes, the scent of mesquite over his lawn. He smiled and shook his head. Maggie shrugged.

"You know," Foley said, casting a glance over Maggie's head at the smoker, "I never got over what you told me about the fox."

Maggie squinted and looked behind her. She called to

one of the small boys who had wandered near the smoker. "That's hot, Ryan," she said. "Don't touch." The boy snapped his head up, looked at the smoker and nodded.

"What fox?" Maggie said, turning back to him.

"The fox I hit with that old Chevrolet," he said. "Before Sophie was born, when I had all the bad luck."

"You hit a fox?" Maggie said.

Foley nodded. Inside the house he could hear that his Nick, his baby boy, had been brought out for a look. "Look at all that hair!" someone said.

"You told me it started my bad luck," he said. "You told me that the fox is a mischief animal."

Maggie laughed. "I did not." She moved to step by him. This time he blocked her way.

"You did," Foley said. "You told me that."

She put her hand on his arm and laughed again. "I'm sorry, but I'm sure I made that up. I was into that magic stuff then. I liked thinking that I knew everything."

Foley felt his eyes widen. "You lied?"

Maggie stiffened a little. "Maybe," she said. "It sounds like a lie, doesn't it?"

Foley was silent.

Maggie was annoyed. "I don't even remember. Maybe it wasn't me. Maybe you just made this up." He said nothing. Maggie said his name, shrugged and went inside. "I was trying to help," she said from around the corner.

"It's okay," he said when she was past him. He lifted a tray from a glass table. The news that she had lied didn't make him mad. He tried to begin the list again as he lifted the lid to the smoker, but he couldn't. It had no beginning.

The children circled around when the smoke cleared. "What are those?" one of them asked, pointing at the foil-wrapped potatoes. "Chicken!" shouted another. "Is that a barbecue?" asked a tiny girl. "Where's the charcoal?" At first, he tried to answer their questions as he forked out the food onto his tray, but then he let them talk, their voices rising up all around him. A few of the older kids helped him carry the food inside. As they entered the house Foley laughed and raised the plate of ribs for all to see. A cheer went up. There was much backslapping, and a toast, to the great good fortune of his family.

Foley as Crabman

C edar Key was polluted by horseshoe crabs that summer. Standing on the dried-out wharf, Foley heard them below him fighting for space in the warm shallows. Their stench hung in the air, warm and dense like the rot of garbage. He leaned against the rail and looked down at them hoisting themselves upward weakly, then falling back, still again. Around them the water rose silently in waves.

No one in town knew why the crabs had come in such great numbers. They covered the beach like a dark blanket. Farther south, Foley had heard, they lay in long piles that spiked out from the shore like sinister boat landings. He lit a cigarette and turned to walk into town. The streets were empty. A sandy white road curled from the wharf and joined the paved road that ran under a stand of cedar trees. Past these trees there stood several bleached-out buildings: a hardware store, a sewing shop, a deserted gas station, a Salvation Army center and the Grand Hotel. As he walked, Foley looked at his shoes—alligator skin, freshly oiled. The fine dust of crushed seashells collected around the eyelets, in the tight places near the soles. In his front pocket, tossing loosely with each step, was a picture of Sophie at the beach in Tarpon Springs. In the picture she held a living sponge, one that Foley had bought from a Greek teenager on the docks. Foley reached in and ran his hand along the edge of the photograph. A force of nervous habit. He never left home without a photograph in his pocket. He pulled them out constantly, with his change, his keys. Often he lost them, but this didn't faze him. He kept a dresserful at home.

He stopped in the shade of the cedar trees and felt the urge to swim. He looked to the swarming beach, the landscape of crabs, and shivered. Maybe he would look at tools.

From out of the hardware store walked a long-legged black man wearing a filthy baseball cap, a blue T-shirt that read MAD BEACH, red shorts and a pair of black work boots. He was the first person Foley had seen on the streets all day. The man walked to the Grand Hotel, peered in the window and ducked inside the screen door. Foley was hungry; he decided to get some turtle soup, a specialty of the Grand Hotel. He walked across the street and pushed on the door, which swung open easily. In the window was a black felt sign with a quarter moon in the lower corner that read "We make the best hamburgers, day or night." Foley stepped into the moist heat of the restaurant.

"Leave it open," said someone behind the bar, someone whom Foley could not see. He squinted. "Leave it that way," he heard.

In the air Foley could smell three things—smoke, hickory he figured, coming from outside, behind the kitchen; sawdust, lying loose and damp on a long shuffleboard table to his right; and a third smell, above the other two somehow, dominating them without obscuring them, ripe, green in the air, plainly turtle soup. As his eyes adjusted, Foley

saw the black man at the end of the bar, leaning over a
newspaper. A woman stood up behind the bar and looked
at Foley.

"You come about the crabs?"

Foley walked to the bar. "I came for soup."

"What about the crabs?" the woman asked. The black
man turned a page.

Foley shrugged. "I don't know anything about them,"
he said.

"Nobody does," said the black man, without looking
up from his paper.

"Somebody does, Piper," the woman said, wiping at
the bar.

"That's what they're sending him for." She turned to
Foley. "Supposed to be here today."

Foley sat down at the bar. "I'm here for the soup," he
said. "I'll take a bowl of turtle soup."

The black man laughed loudly. "Ha!" The woman
shook her head and wiped the back of her hand along her
pale forehead. "It ain't ready," she said.

The black man, Piper, laughed again. "Ha!" It sounded
like a laugh meant to mock something, someone, although
Foley could not be sure what or whom. He looked past
Piper, out the small window at the back of the restaurant to
the Gulf. The barrier islands burned in the sun like thin strips
of ribbon.

"If not for the crabs," Piper said finally, "then why you
here?"

"I'm working on the museum," Foley said. "I came up
from St. Petersburg."

Piper sniffed and bent back over his paper. "You gotta
wait for the soup," he said. "It ain't gonna be ready till
tomorrow."

"I'm leaving today."

"Well, that's a whole lotta too bad," Piper said. "It ain't ready. Soup's gotta cook all day and all night. Simple."

"Simple?" Foley said.

"Simple as that," Piper said.

Foley sighed. "Are you the owner?"

"Ha!" Piper laughed again and was quiet. Foley ran his hand along the ragged edge of the bar. Why couldn't he have soup? It was cooking. He smelled it. Something else was cooking too, out back, over the hickory. My mouth is aching, Foley wanted to say. Let me have the soup.

The woman wiped the bar again. Outside a truck shuddered to a stop in front of the hardware store. Foley asked for a beer and she poured him a draft. When she put it down in front of him, she did not let go. Her hand remained clamped to the glass. She stared at Foley's face as if, given time, she might recognize him. Foley smiled, shifted in his seat.

"Those your teeth?" she asked, squinting a little before Foley put his hand to his mouth. With his other hand, he pulled the beer from her grip.

Foley coughed. "No."

"Didn't think so," she said. "Nice plates though." She bent a little to get a better look. Foley closed his mouth. At thirteen the lymph glands in his neck had become infected. His neck swelled. His face grew round and tight for a week, then turned yellow and hollow for two more. One day his teeth fell out. Into his soup. Swallowed. Lost beneath his bed. "Save those teeth," the dentist told his mother. But Foley took them from a drawer in her room and pushed them down deep into the mud in the back yard. Since then he had been fitted with new dentures every three years.

The woman spoke to him as she bent down behind the bar. "I had an uncle who used to cut plates for a dentist over in Mystic. That's how I knew. I seen a lot of plates. The ones you got there are very good."

She stood up with a bottle of Daiquiri mix. Foley sipped his beer. His teeth always embarrassed him. Each successive plate was different from the last, the teeth longer, or whiter, or farther apart. The change was obvious only to those who knew him well, but so often it seemed the conversations of entire dinners centered on his mouth. People, it seemed, were always bending a little to get a better look at his teeth.

"You want something to eat?" the woman asked him.

"Yes," Foley said. "Turtle soup."

"It isn't ready," the woman said.

"That's what I told him," Piper said without looking up.

"Stay out of it, Piper," the woman said.

"I'll take it even if it isn't cooked all the way," Foley said.

"Can't do that," said the woman.

"Can't do that," Piper echoed.

Foley rolled his eyes. "Look, I've come a long way for the soup. I've had it here before. I want some now." He felt cornered, unsure of what fueled his resistance.

"You can't eat it yet," said the woman, turning her back to him. She pulled out a menu from beside the register. "We got great burgers."

Foley put his hand flat on the bar and took a deep breath. "Since when is there a hard and fast rule about turtle soup?" Out back, the hickory fire picked up in the wind. The smoke blew in and filled the bar. The woman was silent.

Piper snickered. "Yeah, since when is there a hard and fast rule?" he said, pinching and straining his voice to mock Foley's tone.

Throwing her hands into the air, the woman turned to Piper and said, "A rule's a rule. I just do what I'm told about the goddamned soup. You tell him. It's your rule, not mine. I'm sick of telling people the soup's got to cook. It's your rule, so you tell him."

Piper squinted and stood. Foley tensed. Plainly he should have shut up about the soup. As Piper walked over to his stool, Foley opened his mouth to apologize.

"The soup isn't ready," said Piper, stooping a little to bring his face level with Foley's. His breath smelled like old coffee. "I got mullet out back," he said, jerking a thumb over his shoulder, not moving his head. "The mullet's ready. You want one-day soup, then make it yourself. Get the meat from Little Wilson. He got lots of Ridleys these days." He turned from Foley and sat down, running his hand along the brim of his cap. "You make it," he said. "I don't make no one-day soup. My soup cook two days."

Foley stared at him for a moment and then asked the woman, "Who's Little Wilson?" The woman took his glass and filled it without saying anything. "I want some turtle meat," Foley said. Piper smiled without turning his head. The woman set the beer down in front of him and winked at Foley. Behind the hotel the fire crackled loudly.

"I'll take some mullet too," Foley said, louder this time, to break the silence.

Piper turned and walked to a far corner, where he dropped a quarter into a dimly lit jukebox. "The mullet you can have now," he said. "Little Wilson's out on the boat, though. Can't get the turtle meat till he's back. Won't be back till dark."

The woman loudly scooped a glassful of ice. The music started, low and full of bass, as if it were being played in another room. All of this felt important to Foley now. He would wait, he knew. He would put the meat in a cooler and take it home in the back seat. Grace would have recipes.

"Can you wait?" said Piper, hunched over the jukebox, his back still to Foley.

The door to the bar swung open suddenly. A fat man wearing a wide red tie stood in the doorway. Behind him was a policeman, who stared up the street, into the sun. The fat man looked from the bartender to Foley to Piper, breathless. "Is he here for the crabs?"

The woman looked at Foley. "He's the mayor," she said softly.

"No," she shouted to the mayor, "he's eating Piper's mullet. He says he works for the museum."

"Where's the crabman?" said the mayor, shaking his head. Foley took a mouthful of beer. The mayor turned on his heel and slammed back out the door.

"Can you wait?" Piper repeated.

Foley swallowed the beer. "Sure," he said, "for the turtle meat I can wait."

"He thinks they're like roaches," the woman said. She reached up and pulled a string that lit a neon beer sign in the window. "They're crabs. Crabs ain't roaches. These things happen all the time. This town just happens to be here when this thing is happening in this place. It's like a red tide. Can't be stopped."

Piper walked out the back door.

"How long have they been here?" Foley asked.

"A month," the woman said. "Since summer began. They were here before that, all right, but not so thick as now. Never seen 'em so thick. Some think it's a sign of a hurricane summer. Piper thinks they're giving up 'cause of all the gas and oil in the water. Piper thinks it's just their time to quit."

Piper entered the back door with a plate full of twisted yellow mullet fillets. "You want a fork?" he asked Foley, setting the plate before him. He slapped a fork on the counter before Foley could answer.

"I take you to Little Wilson at eight-thirty. You driving," he said. "You still want to wait?"

Foley said that he did, and Piper turned, picked up his

paper, and walked out the door. The woman topped off Foley's beer and began to swipe her cloth around the door frame. She wiped her way into the kitchen, where Foley could hear her, over the rattles of fishing boats out on the water, over the sound of the jukebox dropping a disc back into place.

Foley spent the afternoon in the old museum, bent over the curator's sketches, a dusty window air conditioner blowing cold air on his sweaty back. At three-fifteen he called Grace, told her he would be late and talked to Sophie. "Daddy," she told him, "Nick scratched all your records with a fork."

At five-fifteen Foley walked back to the Grand Hotel and started in on the food and beer. He talked a good while with the bartender, whose name was Sara. She brought him mullet and poured him beers, complained about the crabs and the heat and the delays in the plans to pave Cedar Key's roads. She gave him a pamphlet, "Be Upbeat and Beat Up Stress," at eight o'clock, just as the sun set over the barrier islands, and the wind shifted, blowing in the smell of the crabs with the darkness. Foley read the pamphlet. He was a little drunk and not getting much out of it when Piper appeared at the door.

"Mr. Turtle Meat," he said. "What's your name?"

"Foley. Dan Foley."

"Well, Daniel, you going to meet Little Wilson. Let's go."

Piper said nothing as they drove out of town, east at first, toward Chiefland, and then south, along a straight, deserted highway. Foley broke the silence by asking how much the turtle meat would cost.

"It cost what Little Wilson ask for it," he said. "Different every time."

Piper's silence and seeming antagonism made Foley uncomfortable. He felt as if he were being led into an ambush.
Suddenly he was unsure why he had decided to trust this
man who now stared out into the night through his open
window, spitting occasionally toward the pine forest that ran
like black curtains along both sides of the road. Finally after
ten miles or so the landscape began to break up. Foley saw
inlets on his right and low, hilly fields to the left. Soon he
saw lights from small fishing boats on the inlet, and this
comforted him. Then Piper said, "Pull over in the motel."

Foley saw no motel and drove past the point where
Piper wanted him to turn. Piper threw an arm out the window and said loudly, "The motel! The motel!" Foley slowed
and circled back into a small gravel parking lot that fronted
on a series of wooden shacks. There was no light in the
parking lot and Foley's headlights revealed only a rusted-out
golf cart in the weeds at the edge of the lot and a wall of
fishing nets strung from the side of the nearest shack.

Piper stared out the window past the shacks. "See the
light?" he said. "Little Wilson's out back with the Ridleys."

After turning off his headlights, Foley could indeed see
a light, a dim blue light that appeared like a dome over the
shacks. It hung in the air like the light of a distant city. Piper
opened his door and stepped out. Foley did the same. Piper
was a silhouette against the blackness of the night. Foley
struggled to distinguish the outlines of his clothes as he
moved. He followed Piper to the first shack.

"Little Wilson!" Piper called out into the darkness.

From somewhere beyond the shacks there came a reply.
"I don't want you, crabman. Go away."

"It ain't the crabman. It Piper, and I brought someone
for the turtle meat. Someone thinks he can make the soup
hisself. He coming back. Don't you shoot him!"

There was no reply this time. Foley put his hand in his

pocket and reached for the picture of Sophie. "Is this guy dangerous?" he asked Piper.

"Hell no," said Piper, "he just don't like surprises. He nervous sometimes. Simple."

Foley watched Piper and thought of starting back but waited instead for Piper's first move. In the distance a cicada started in.

"Go on," said Piper finally.

"Alone?" Foley asked. "What about you?"

"I going home," he said. "I live 'round here."

Foley listened to a distant hum, a faraway highway or a boat on the Gulf. Then he heard the faint sound of singing, Little Wilson he supposed, somewhere out there in the light.

"What you nervous 'bout, Mr. Daniel?"

Foley looked at Piper. "I don't even know where I am," he said. "I can't even see the car from here."

Piper laughed. "Truth is," he said, "I was going to take some money off you for this. Now I ain't going to."

Foley's hands were shaking. "Are you going to steal my car?"

"No," Piper said, "I got a car. Go get the meat. Tell Little Wilson to turn on the lights out here when you leave. Go back out the same way you came."

The whole thing was a setup. Piper was going to take the car. Little Wilson, that distant singer, would blast him for the money. The woods held little hope of escape. Foley felt suffocated by the heat, by the voice of Piper, by the sound of the insects, by his own foolishness. He felt a hand on his shoulder. "Why you trust me so?"

Foley's knees weakened. He recalled Grace once telling him to grow up after he was mugged in Miami. Afterward he had walked around in a cloud, fearful, always questioning. "You're such a victim, Foley," she'd said. "You're not the only one taking a beating around here." Thoughts of

turning and punching Piper, of bowling him over, of flailing
out and beating him with his fists, passed over him. What
was there to hit? Piper was disembodied by the blackness.

"Trust?" Foley said. "What's not to trust?"

"Ha!" Piper laughed loudly, slapping his hand on Foley's back, genuinely laughing for the first time all day. "I'm
not to trust, Mr. Daniel. The little man with the turtles is
not to trust. But you got what you want. You want soup.
You want turtle meat. You got to trust what you want."

Foley prepared himself for a blow. Piper's hand left
his back.

"Go back and get it," Piper said. "It's all right. Anybody wants soup bad as you going to be okay with Little
Wilson. Long as you pay."

Foley turned. He saw Piper's shape moving off into the
woods.

"Go on back, fool. Don't wait forever. He forget I
called back to him and then he shoot you for sure."

He disappeared into the woods. Foley considered going
back to the car, but he decided to get the meat and leave
fast. As he walked around the shacks and the tall cedar fence
behind them, he came to another group of buildings, bungalows, arranged in a semicircle; beyond it was the blackness
of the inlet. The bungalows were dingy, washed-out struc-
tures. Foley looked for movement in them. Above the door
of the farthest one, a yellow bug light burned vacantly in
the night. In the center of the semicircle was a swimming
pool from which rose the grand blue light they had seen
from the parking lot. At first Foley thought it was empty,
but soon he heard splashings and the sonorous echo of humming. He walked to the edge of the pool and looked down
into the harsh light. The bottom was covered in a black
muck, which had splashed up onto the walls of the deep end
in ribbons and drips. In the center of the deep end, knee deep

in black water, stood a very small man, a dwarf actually, looking up at Foley. Little Wilson.

"If you're a crabman," said Little Wilson, his voice amplified by the walls of the pool, "then you can get out now."

Foley shook his head. "I'm an architect," he said. "I want some turtle meat." Around his ears small bugs buzzed and darted. In the air he smelled dead fish and the bitterness of chlorine. The little man began to laugh and a cicada, hooked under a poolside lawn chair, blasted the night air. When Foley jumped at the sound, Little Wilson laughed louder. His short arms were heavily muscled. He wore only overalls and black boots that rose to his hips. Despite his height he was barrel-chested. On his hands he wore pink rubber gloves covered with the black muck.

"It's turtle you want?" he said, kneeling suddenly, slipping his hands down into the muck at his feet. Foley struggled not to look about the fringes of the light for Piper's return. He was unsure of how to make small talk with this dwarf. He swallowed, half expecting Piper to come running out of the night, bolting forward to toss him down into the blackness at the bottom of the pool. "I wanted soup," Foley said. "They told me it wasn't ready yet. So I came to get my own meat."

Suddenly the dwarf grumbled and stood lifting a black turtle high above his head. Looking closer at the bottom of the pool, Foley began to see that it was alive with movement just beneath the surface. He could see the light reflecting off the dark humps of other turtles and could now hear their splashings. He stepped back from the edge. What he smelled in the air was turtles; the blackness was their blood.

The dwarf walked to the shallow end, where his movements became measured and precise. He laid the turtle on its back on the top step. He then turned and walked back to the edge of the muck, which formed sort of a shoreline where the deep end fell away. He knelt again and circled his hands in the shallow water there, feeling for something. Looking up at Foley, the dwarf squinted in the bright light and said, "Ridleys are sweet." As he said it, his hands settled on something. Smiling broadly he pulled a small hatchet from below. It was as long as his right arm. Turning on his heels, he walked back to the shallow end, where he took off a glove and carefully wiped the blood off the underside of the turtle.

"Are you sure you ain't a health man?" he said softly as he worked.

"No, I'm an architect," Foley replied. The dwarf bent and scratched a line on the belly of the turtle with the edge of the hatchet.

"I've had health men here," he said without looking up. "They closed down my motel. Said I was a hazard using the pool like this. Hell, no one cared when I used the pool to raise baitfish. The customers liked it. No one closed me down then."

Foley walked around and stood above him in the shallow end.

"Now they're saying I put the nets across the inlets." His face was brightly lit by the pool light, a sheen of sweat and blood across his forehead and cheeks. To Foley he looked like a photograph now, the aqua-blue walls of the pool defining his face. His fingers locked on the handle of the hatchet. "The crabman said I poured oil along the nets and that's what's keeping the crabs out and the turtles in. I did no such thing. I've always trapped Ridleys and I never netted the inlets. But they came around here testing my water, checking my catch, searching my boat. I told them, 'Crabs is the town's problem.' They say it killed off the town having them crabs rolling in like big brown waves underneath the wharf." He spit. "Hell, I say the town never had no golden age anyways."

Foley shrugged. "They sure stink, though."

"That'll pass," Little Wilson said. He raised the hatchet. "Stinks always pass," he said, slamming the hatchet down into the belly of the turtle. The shell cracked loudly and the turtle stretched its legs, spasmed, and died. Foley looked away, at his shoes; a streak of blood ran across his toes. Little Wilson pulled a screwdriver from his back pocket and worked the hatchet loose from the shell. Turning the turtle up on its side, he pushed his hand into the hole left by the hatchet and pulled at the shell until it cracked and came away, exposing the turtle's pink and black innards. Little Wilson tucked his hand under the body of the turtle and pulled it free from the shell in one tug. The turtle now lay limply over the dwarf's small hand, whole but for its shell, head and feet dangling.

Foley's chest tightened. The turtle looked too much like a small child in the tiny man's hand. The dwarf lobbed the shell out into the tall grass by the inlet and threw the body into a bucket at the top of the stairs. He climbed up and, pulling off the gloves, offered his hand to Foley.

"You want frozen or fresh?" he said to Foley.

"I don't much care," Foley said.

"I'll give you frozen then," Little Wilson said. "It won't smell as bad." He turned from Foley and walked to the nearest bungalow. Before going in, he turned and yelled to Foley, "I'll give you five pounds for thirty bucks." Foley nodded and Little Wilson went inside.

Standing alone at the edge of the pool, he felt the urge to walk. He moved toward the inlet. Somehow he felt beaten. As he dragged his shoes through the tall grass, he saw that the ground was littered with turtle shells. Hundreds of them. He stepped around them until they were too thick to avoid. The light of the pool faded as he approached the inlet. The shells tipped and clattered under his feet.

He was alone, far from his car, even farther from his home and children; his stumblings seemed the only force that propelled him. His shoes slipped from shell to toppling shell, feet always moving forward blindly. How had he come to be here? He tried to remember and was angry that he could not. The soup, the turtle meat meant nothing to him.

At the water's edge he kicked something softer and lighter than a turtle shell. He bent over to get a look. A horseshoe crab. He lifted it up from the shady bank and held it by its long horn. In the dim light from the pool, the underside of the crab looked dry and delicate. Its legs twitched and a thin brown liquid dripped from the bottom of the shell.

Foley barely heard the blast from behind him before he felt his back and neck sting terribly. He lurched forward, almost dropping the crab. He bent a little and turned. Little Wilson, silhouetted by the light that rose from the pool, stood holding a shotgun that was longer than his entire body. Foley reached up and put a hand to his neck. Warmth. Blood.

"That's rock salt, you damn crabman," Little Wilson yelled. "Next barrel ain't rock salt. It's something worse."

Foley didn't speak. He looked again at the crab, its legs pulled tight to its body in fear. This is prehistoric, he thought. This should have been extinct long ago.

"I knew you were a crabman," Little Wilson said. "I had you pegged. You didn't want turtle meat. I could tell. Why would you come all this way for frozen turtle meat?"

"I don't know," said Foley, still holding the crab up.

" 'Cause you're a crabman, that's why!" Little Wilson shouted, raising the shotgun up with considerable effort. "You want to take what little I got. You're supposed to be helping people, but instead you're out here blaming me, lying to me, telling me you are what you ain't. You come poking around in what you don't know, what you don't care about. Damn you, put that thing down."

Foley lifted the crab a little higher and turned toward the water. He took a last look at it, reached back and lobbed it out over the inlet. It disappeared into the night air before he heard the splash. He then turned, raised his hands so that Little Wilson wouldn't shoot him, and walked carefully back through the turtle shells without saying anything. Little Wilson hoisted the shotgun and circled around behind him, poking the barrel into his ribs. Foley walked through the grass to the pool, stopping at the edge, looking down at the turtles in the blackness.

Foley knew, without turning to look, that Little Wilson was crying and that out in the water the crab he had held for those moments was digging down into the cool mud. In front of him was the pool, filled with black blood and turtles. Behind him was Little Wilson, pushing the shotgun into his ribs, chiding him.

"You don't fool me. You're a crabman. Say it. You're the crabman and you're scared. Say it!"

"Yes," Foley said. "I am that. I am the crabman." He felt himself moving then, walking into the blackness and the night with no hope of escape.

Foley's
Rapture

A t one point Foley decided to do something about his lying. Why was he so fond of it? The question consumed his days. At dinner he would feel the urge to tell a story, a lie. Other hams sliced. The first ham. The ham crunch. People nodded, chewed, raised eyebrows. He felt that his tales inspired them.

He never lied to his children, although he told them stories about the bears he had seen as a boy in the Adirondacks, where he had spent his summers. Once he claimed to have been a boxer—which was a lie—until Nick, who was five at the time, kicked him in the face in sort of a challenge.

"How do you stop that, Daddy?"

Foley, who had been watching television with Sophie, squeezed Nick's knee until his eyes cleared. It took some time, since Nick had caught him flush in the nose, and later he remembered hearing Sophie shouting to Grace, "Daddy's squeezing Nick's leg off!" and thinking that the whole thing was his fault, the result of another one of his lies.

Once it happened that he was caught in a lie and there

was really very little for him to do about it. "Why did you tell Max Webber you could scuba-dive?" Grace asked him one dim November evening, just before they left for a party up in Tarpon Springs. She leaned to the left and twisted an earring. Foley, who was shaving, thought it a strange gesture, as if she were regarding herself in a mirror, yet she was facing him.

"I could scuba-dive," he said, lifting the blade from his face. She smirked. He gritted his teeth, pulled his face with the razor. "If I wanted to, I could get certified. It doesn't take much."

"Sarah tells me they want to invite us out on that damned boat this weekend," she said. *"This* weekend."

"That's easy," Foley said. "We can't. We can be busy."

In the living room Nick and Sophie were fighting. "Never, never, never!" Sophie yelled.

Grace picked up a hairbrush. "You can't get around this," she said. "You lie to Max, so we have to stay home. What if he wants to borrow your equipment? What then?"

"I never said anything about equipment," Foley said, bending close to the mirror, hoping the conversation might drift off and die. Grace stood in the doorway and put dabs of perfume on her wrists. She looked down, checked her fingers. Foley thought nothing about the fact that she was quiet for a moment, that her gestures were cold.

"The hell you didn't," Grace said.

"I'm telling you I didn't," Foley said, pushing his chin out.

"You did."

He only vaguely remembered the conversation with Max. It had begun with a discussion of nitrogen narcosis and aircraft decompression. Something was said about "rapture of the deep."

"Have you ever had it?" Max had asked him. They

were drinking beer out of mason jars at a bar they liked called the Old Salt.

"When?"

"When you dive?" Max said.

That confused Foley. Had he lied or had Max simply implanted the story for him to carry on? He couldn't remember his answer. He had mumbled a few words about regulators.

Now he turned to Grace. "I wasn't drunk."

She lifted a foot and peeled a banana sticker off the heel of her shoe. "So?" she said, without looking at him. She tugged the hem of her dress, pressed down on her stomach, and softly said, "Fat," as if Foley weren't there to hear her. In the front hall the kids slammed the desk drawers open and shut wildly. Nick shouted, "Mints!" Foley heard their hands sloshing around in his change jar. Grace seemed not to notice this, either.

"I don't think anything was said about equipment," Foley said. Why was he so fuzzy?

"That's what I'm telling you," Grace said, looking up at him. "You did. You told him you had equipment. He's been talking about it for a month. He wants us to go out on the boat. I'm going."

When had they talked? A month ago? Foley had seen Max three days ago while driving past a liquor store in Madeira Beach. When Max waved, he slowed the car and waved back. Then Max put his hand behind his back, fanned it out, and wiggled his ass. Foley laughed and drove on, not having the slightest idea what Max was doing. Now he knew . . . Max was a fish. They were going diving.

"Shit," Foley said.

He wiped his face with a towel and thought. Grace reached out and put a hand on his belly. "Tell him you lied."

Foley saw no choice. Just then Sophie leaned in the

bathroom door. "Excuse me," she said, somewhat pointedly. "Daddy, the mint man came. Do you want a mint?"

It had become Sophie's habit recently to ignore Grace. Foley tried hard not to fancy himself the favorite, as he could clearly remember the time Nick rushed past him to Grace when Ginger, the family shepherd, was slammed into Gulf Boulevard by a station wagon full of Mormons. If Sophie had nothing but contempt for her mother, it was because she was twelve. "Your time will come," Grace told him.

"I think I own the whole box," he said.

"Stop it, Daddy," she said, sliding back around the door frame.

"Tell him you lied," Grace said again.

Foley turned on the faucet. The cold water brought courage to mind, morning, the human spirit. For a moment he felt resolve. "I'll have to," he said, with his forehead against the mirror. "I'll have to tell him the truth." Then Grace kissed him on the shoulder.

But driving to work the next day Foley went the long way just to pass the marina. He told himself it was for the drive, but he knew what he was doing: looking for a way out, a cheap scuba school or secondhand equipment, although he had little real hope. He pulled off the highway and drove under a bridge at the inlet, past three large tourist fishing boats. He stopped the car near a sign that read TANKS FILLED and for an instant this seemed to be the most obvious place to be, as if nothing other than whim had compelled him to come here.

It was still early, and the sun was just cracking over the rooftops. Beyond the sign, which was tacked to a telephone pole, there stood a tiny building with a flatbed trailer and a filthy director's chair in front of it. A cardboard box—one that once held a washing machine—stood in the center of the trailer. In the distance Foley heard the sound of a heavy motor revving out on the bay. He turned off the car's engine and took a deep breath.

Foley knew of scuba schools, and he knew that he could probably hold Max off. On the way out he had kept telling himself, "I'm not stupid." With a phone call to Max this could all be over. What he feared most was the scant moment of disbelief he knew would pass over Max's face when he told him he had lied about the whole thing. It was too easy for him to foresee Max slapping an understanding paw on his shoulder, laughing with him, guiding him by the elbow through his office waiting room or across some parking lot. Max, the guide now, thinking, as he rubbed Foley's shoulder just the tiniest bit, "He's lying for me. For me."

Truly that was what Foley feared. So even if he felt criminal for sneaking off, spending money to avoid embarrassment, it was simpler somehow this way. Painless.

He stepped out of the car and flipped down his sunglasses. The heat had not yet begun, and the wharf, where he brought Nick on weekends to pick up grouper steaks, seemed alien to him. "Wednesday," he said aloud, as if that explained it. At the door of the building, he reached through the rusty screen and knocked. No one answered. He glanced around behind him, then looked in the window, pressing close to get past the glare. There was a long counter inside and not much else: another director's chair, a stack of newspapers, and a cash register with the drawer open. Empty boxes, the kind auto parts come in, littered the floor.

He was about to give up when he saw movement through the window at the back of the building. An old man stood staring at the ground below the window. Foley waved, but the man, obviously absorbed by whatever lay there,

didn't notice. It occurred to Foley that the man might be
trying to break in, and, after a moment of standing there
awkwardly, he tried to slide out of his line of vision, but the
man suddenly straightened and walked away from the window. Foley tensed, turned for the car. Just as he reached for
his keys, he heard footsteps around the side of the shed and
a voice.

"Can you give me a hand with this pumpkin?"

Foley turned to find the man standing at the corner of
the building, holding a fishnet in his hand. He had dark skin,
muddled by patches of darker brown concentrated around
the bridge of his nose and along the ridge above his eyebrows. His hair was white, cut short and tight to the head.
His T-shirt said NASTY GIRLS in airbrush stencil.

He spoke again without waiting for an answer. "I can't
find my boy and it's too heavy for just an old man. Have
you seen it?"

Foley jingled the change in his pockets. "What?"

"The beauty," the old man said, putting a leg up and
climbing onto the trailer. "The prize."

Foley squinted and glanced sideward. In the distance a
little boy held an eel up to the cars that drove by on the
drawbridge.

"Look," the old man said, standing with his hands on
the edge of the washing-machine box. "Look at the prize."

Foley climbed up onto the trailer, with the old man
coaxing him along. When he stood on top of the trailer bed,
the sun came directly over the rooftop and hit him square in
the face. He shaded his eyes. The old man smelled like a tin
ashtray. Wedged in the box was a truly gigantic pumpkin,
which Foley immediately reached down to and touched.
"Lord," he said, wanting right away to take it back to Nick
and Sophie.

The old man smiled broadly. "The beauty."

"Where did you get it?" Foley said, rubbing away at the dirt stuck to the hide of the pumpkin with his thumbnail.

"My sister," said the man, without looking up. He began unfolding the net. "She grew it."

"Where does she live?"

The old man stopped. "Does it matter? She gave it to me." He reached into his pocket and ceremoniously pulled out a pack of cigarettes. "I didn't steal it."

"I'm sure you didn't," Foley said. "I just wondered how she did it."

"Well, she did it," the old man said sharply. He lit his cigarette, then crumpled the pack and threw it into the carton on top of the pumpkin. "Are you helping me?"

Foley realized he was late for work, but the thought struck him like a distant message. He had too many reasons to forget work: somehow he believed he might just yet learn to scuba-dive today; he had to see this pumpkin whole; Max might call. Besides, there was always the chance of cheap fish on the wharf. He could rent a rod, wait for the charters to come in.

He nodded. "Sure, I'll help you out."

The old man snorted and reached down into the box with the net in his fist. "Grab it," he said to Foley. "We gotta lift her out. I put bricks in the bottom of the box so it wouldn't tip over. Now I can't budge it."

Foley reached into the carton, edged the net beneath the pumpkin, and pulled it taut. The old man grunted and together they heaved it up to the top of the box, where it stuck for a moment. The weight was considerable, and the old man moaned, "Oh, sweet Jesus," with his cigarette pinched in a corner of his mouth. Only the fear that the pumpkin might slip and plummet down on top of the pile of bricks kept Foley holding tight. His ribs ached as they heaved again and again, trying in vain to lift the pumpkin over the final six inches. At one point they let it rest on the corner of the box as Foley got a better grip on the net. The old man slapped the pumpkin and called it a whore just as Foley lifted suddenly, jerking the pumpkin into a tighter wedge and, for an instant, raising the whole box off the ground.

The pumpkin was stuck. As they both relaxed, the box leaned and bent, and the old man fell to his knees to hold it there. "Get the snips," he said, grunting. "Go inside and get my tin snips from behind the bar. We can cut it out."

Foley jumped down off the trailer. The old man was breathing heavily, so he jogged to the door and twisted the handle. The door swung open, and a metallic smell blew out to Foley. Several welding tanks stood strapped to one wall, and opposite them stood a counter on top of which rested eight perfect wedges of fresh white apple and a light patina of sawdust and salt. Foley walked behind the bar, eyeing the apple with some suspicion, and looked around for the tin snips. He found them in a shoe box full of tools, grabbed them, and walked back out to the old man.

A thought struck him as he stepped out into the sun: where's the scuba equipment? Before he could turn back to take a second look, he saw the old man lying flat on his back on the trailer. The box had tilted completely now and the pumpkin had spilled almost all the way out. It rested awkwardly between the man's legs, which were spread around it.

"Are you all right?" Foley shouted. He ran to the trailer and slapped the tin snips down. The man's eyes were closed. His head rolled slightly. "My arm," he said. "My arm hurts."

"Is it broken?" Foley said, thinking more about the pumpkin. He put his hand on the man's shoulder. "Which one?"

"My balls," the old man said. "I'm dying."

Foley climbed up onto the trailer and carefully pulled

the box away from the man, until the pumpkin slipped free. It thudded down on the rusty iron bed of the trailer, and, with his eyes screwed, the old man looked between his raised knees at Foley, who reached down and settled the pumpkin into place.

The old man rolled over on his side, with both hands folded between his thighs. "Do you need a doctor?" Foley said.

"Not hardly." His breaths were short and dry. Foley could see a bank clock on a building across the inlet, and a small plane flying over it. He reached to hand the old man his handkerchief, tapping him lightly on the shoulder. The man's T-shirt was pulled up around the middle of his back, exposing that region of flesh, that roll of fat around the lower back, which for Foley always brought to mind his father. His father's sweaters and shirts always crept up his back, giving young Foley flashes of skin at the most unexpected times—as he piled wood in January, for instance, or reached down into an engine for an oily bolt dropped on top of some nameless assembly. The old man's skin was light brown, unlike his father's, but marked by the same translucence, the same spotting, even the same scattering of moles. As the old man started to roll from side to side in preparation for raising himself up, Foley remembered his father shooting baskets with Hank and him in the middle of winter, on a backboard he had bought at a public-school auction and had thrown up on the side of the house the same day. His father's shot was awkward, almost palsied, and Foley burned with embarrassment for him with each shot. *For* him, he remembered telling his mother later; he was embarrassed *for* him, not *by* him. "If he can't shoot, why doesn't he just forget about it?" he asked her. While they shot, Hank taunted his father. "Your gut's hanging, Dad." His father grunted to indicate concentration. Head back, chin pointed, he lifted the ball up and with a strange fluttering push shot it again and again, missing each time.

Finally the two brothers lost interest and left their father out at the side of the house shooting for the basket. At dinnertime he came in, his hands stiff and black from the skin of mud on the wet leather ball. "I just made six in a row," he said, running his hands under cold water to lose the numbness. The rest of them were at the table. Hank rolled his eyes, plainly skeptical. "Six in a row," his father said again, as he sat. "That's the truth." Later Hank told Foley their father was a liar. Foley protested. They argued late into the night, from one bed to the other. Foley never saw his father touch a basketball again. The argument was never settled. When he finally learned Hank was tending bar in Colorado, he went to tell him news of their father's death and they argued it one more time. "Six in a row, my ass," Hank said. "Look, he was an undertaker. They make great liars."

The old man stood up and bent over the pumpkin. "We need to lift it," he said. "We need to carry it around back."

It seemed preposterous to Foley that the old man would expect the two of them to be able to carry the pumpkin any distance, but the old man quickly rolled the pumpkin to the edge of the trailer, hopped down and began pulling it toward him. "Come on, grab ahold," he said, slapping hard on the side of the pumpkin. As they slipped it off the trailer, Foley was stunned by the clumsy weight. After only a few steps in unison with the man, he asked for a rest.

"I've been doing this all week," the old man said. "This one's the toughest, but I've been doing it by myself up till now."

Foley didn't believe him. He smirked, and bent at the knees in preparation to pick the pumpkin up again. They lifted together and slowly made their way down the alley beside the shed. Foley got a look inside at one point, and caught a glimpse of a phone. The thought of calling in to work crossed his mind as he slid his feet along the road, but what would he say? How could he explain his absence? He didn't have a story and he knew it. They might have already called Grace to find out where he was. This reassured him, since he knew she would cover for him, but he knew then he'd have to explain to her.

"Do you smoke?" the old man wheezed. The two of them faced each other across the pumpkin as they shuffled it at knee level down the alley. Foley nodded. "Let me have a square then."

They set the pumpkin down and sat on it as Foley reached into his breast pocket for his cigarettes. He was hot, overheated, he knew, and he could feel his heartbeat with the fingers in his pocket. The inlet ran behind the buildings, and the end of the alley, Foley could now see, butted up against a small seawall. Something around the corner smelled heavy and rotten, compounding the lightheadedness Foley was experiencing from the heat and exertion. The buildings on either side of him were sun-bleached and dotted with various salts and lichen. The two men lit their cigarettes off a single match and sat in silence.

On the road, on the drawbridge, the cars hummed by, running the smooth and steady parallel of Gulf Boulevard. The repetition, the slice of each car through the salt air, the heavy pull of the barge horns on the bay flattened the moment, and soon all that seemed to connect Foley to the world was the pumpkin itself. It rocked slowly under the weight of the two men and Foley felt that it was a third presence between them. He scratched his black oxfords in the sand, ground his cigarette out, and waited for the old man to stand up. The man pulled at his T-shirt, wiped his brow, then slid around the pumpkin until he was facing the opposite direction from Foley. Then, somewhat dramatically, he laid his head down on his knees and moaned.

This startled Foley, who stood up quite suddenly and fidgeted in his pockets, until the old man said, "Heartburn. Christ, my heartburn."

"Maybe we ought to leave this here," Foley said, staring at the back of the man's head. On his neck, just below his hairline, and partly obscured by the collar of his shirt, Foley could see some kind of tattoo. "Maybe you ought to go inside and rest."

The old man grumbled and, after pausing in this position, face down, staring straight at the ground between his feet, he threw down his cigarette and stood. "Bullshit," he said. "Let's have some fun."

He clapped his hands, and before Foley had a chance to ask him about the tattoo he was bent back over the pumpkin, heaving it once again. They hauled it around the back of the building on this leg of the trip and set it down in a small sandy area there. A long bench, with several empty cans and five screwdrivers on it, stood just below the window. The back door was closed, although its screen door was propped open by another smaller pumpkin. On the ground, in the stiff grass that grew in patches, were the remains of what looked like twenty or thirty more pumpkins, all in varying states of decay. They were spread evenly, broken and split in pieces of all sizes, like eggshells across the bottom of a sink. Slowly Foley became aware of something else in the air besides the smell of rot. Flies.

"What the hell is this?" he said, unsure of exactly what he was looking at. Carnage. Garbage. Trouble.

"It's my archery range," the old man said, smiling directly at Foley's puzzlement.

Foley didn't take him seriously at first, but then the old man quietly picked up a rather sizable bow from the sand and pointed to a garbage can full of arrows. Foley walked to it and picked one up. It was slick with pumpkin guts. All of them were; still others, Foley found, were crusted with it. He could see now that many of the shards of pumpkin at his feet had a chaotic lattice of small holes in them.

"You want to try it?" the old man said, holding out the bow to him. Foley shook his head.

The old man snorted. He raised the bow up and pulled back hard on the draw, staring straight over his fist, taking a sort of empty aim at Foley. He held like that for a minute, and although the bow was plainly empty, Foley found it uncomfortable to be a potential target. "What are you shooting at?" he said. The old man eased off the draw, and took a deep breath.

"Pumpkins."

Foley laughed. The old man walked to the garbage can, pulled an arrow out, loaded, drew and, before Foley could say a word, fired straight at the giant pumpkin. The arrow breezed low and hard and snapped the skin of the pumpkin, sinking in fully.

"Jesus!" Foley said, thinking the old man must have made a mistake. A motorboat roared by them.

"Try it!" the old man shouted. "It's a gas."

Foley was incredulous. The old man offered up the bow again. Foley waved it away. "Don't waste it," he said.

The old man grinned, spreading his dry lips tight over his teeth. "Waste what?" he said. "It's only a pumpkin. It's nothing valuable. It's not a painting. Pumpkins have no value."

Foley searched his mind for recipes, some justification for not wasting the pumpkin. The old man drew another arrow. "You should try it," he said. "There's nothing like it." He fired. The arrow skidded off the side of the pumpkin and landed harmlessly in the sand beyond it. "My sister didn't want them. They were left over from Halloween. All except this one. This one's the last of them. She wouldn't sell this one."

Foley decided to leave then. He had had enough of the old man. He hated him for destroying the pumpkin, although in truth he couldn't think of anything better to do with it. He could have taken it home with him. There would have been photos. Nick and Sophie wrapping themselves around it lovingly.

As Foley started to say good-bye, the old man bent over and moaned about his heartburn again. He dropped in the sand abruptly, dropping the bow. "Wait a second," he said. "Wait just a second."

Foley could not shake the feeling that the old man was talking to someone else. He bent down and put his hand on the old man's knee. "Are you all right?" he said. The old man looked up, and Foley could see that he was in terrific pain. His face was flushed a deep red, and his eyes were open wide, in a gesture of wonder, or fear, Foley couldn't be sure which. He clutched his chest tightly, balled his T-shirt up in his fist.

Foley felt a rush of panic. "Lean back," he said, reassured by the sound of his own voice. "I'll call the doctor." He stood, took another look at the old man, whose breathing was forced and irregular now, and turned back toward the building. As he went in, out of the sunlight he heard the old man respond in whispers. "Yes, yes."

He thought for a moment of calling Max Webber, but dialed the operator instead. He had a flash just then, in the moment before the operator answered. It was a dream, really, fully developed and complete, in which he called Max and asked him to come out to the marina at once. "Here," he heard himself say, "is my scuba man. Can you help him?" Things could be explained then; his original lie would mean nothing in this equation. Max would bend over the man, bring him up and out, heal him and cool him, and all would be forgotten.

Foley suddenly found that he was yelling into the phone. "Jesus, help," he said. "I need some help here."

The operator switched him to an emergency room, which took a moment and gave him time to despise himself for thinking about Max at all. He held on to the phone, stretched the cord out to its fullest in order to get a look out the door at the old man. Foley could see only his legs. This made him more frantic. "Hello!" he shouted into the phone.

Soon a young doctor was on the line, calming him, giving him instructions, taking his name and the address, which Foley didn't know exactly. "How long?" he said to the doctor.

"Ten minutes, at the outside."

This didn't reassure Foley, but he decided to try to appear as calm as possible as he walked back outside to the man. Right away, though, perhaps even before he turned the corner of the doorway, Foley knew the man was dead. He lay flat and heavy, with his legs splayed something like they were around the pumpkin only minutes before. His skin was pallid, his eyes open and frozen. Foley knelt down over him and pounded his chest, as he had seen others do. He pushed breath in the man's lungs, as calmly and evenly as he could.

The man's mouth tasted like mustard. For an instant Foley forgot a lifetime of kisses and felt amazement that a human being had taste. A man's taste defined him. Here was this sour old man. Mustard. He breathed hard into the man's mouth. Vinegar. He put his head on the man's chest, listened for something. He breathed again. Rotting fruit. Again. Pickled eggs. Again. Upholstery.

Soon he quit, and breathless from the exertion and emotion, he sat next to the old man and waited for the ambulance. It didn't come—at least not right away—and Foley wrapped his arms around his knees and turned his back to the sun to warm himself. He stood, and walked around the man's body. He had seen a lot worse as a boy, but he had never seen anyone die, and the calm in the man's face seemed contradictory to the tension Foley felt. There would be the explanations—to the police, to Grace, to his friends and children. The story would get around; he'd be forced to correct people on the details if the facts were to be kept straight.

"I was there to pick up scuba equipment," he would say. No, not that. "I was there helping this old man move a pumpkin." That seemed right, and it was. It was the truth. He wanted a piece of that, wanted to hold on to it. He looked around to get a good picture of the place, grabbed the old man's leg, touched his cheek, then stood up to look out over the inlet. Freeze this, he thought. Hold this.

He picked up the old man's bow and bounced it in his hand, marveling at its lightness and balance. In the distance, to the north, he heard the ambulance coming toward him now. This released him from the moment and again he could hear the questions from his friends, and could see the story expanding and contracting, the reality of this day all but forgotten.

As the ambulance raced up and over the drawbridge and then straight by the marina and off into the distance again, Foley leaned down and picked up an arrow he found in the sand there. He laid it in place in the bow, drew and fired at the pumpkin. He missed, having aimed too high, and the arrow stuck in the sand beyond it, making a sound like an emery board on thick toenails. The sound gave Foley a chill, as it always did when Grace did her nails in his presence. He walked to the garbage can and pulled out another arrow. He aimed this time, and as he released he knew that the arrow would hit the pumpkin. It flew in a rigid arc, and struck the pumpkin about three quarters of the way down, sinking in about five inches. Foley grabbed another arrow, took three or four steps toward the pumpkin and drew back on the bow as far as he could. His arms wavered; his fingers hurt. He fixed his aim as best he could, and released. The bowstring snapped taut. The arrow was gone. He heard the cut through the air, and the slice of the shaft into the pumpkin. *Thoop.*

He stood for a moment, struck by the physicality of the event. Before, when the old man had fired, it had seemed destructive and arbitrary. But now he was thrilled by all of this. He took another arrow and shot it, striking the side of the pumpkin and catching. The sound seemed less rich than the last shot, so he fired again.

It was a good while before the ambulance arrived, but when it finally did Foley was breathless. He had riddled the pumpkin with arrows, and it lay like a dead animal in the distance, slick arrows protruding chaotically from its hide. Foley heard the ambulance finally make the right turn into the marina. He reached down and wiped the sweat from his hands on his pant legs and set the bow down next to the old man. When the tires of the ambulance finally skidded to a stop on the gravel in front of the shed, Foley looked over the water at the sunlight in the black glass of the office buildings. The brackish waves eased in and out against the cement and the birds barreled down from above. The old man, with his bow at his side, lay in a meadow of sand and pumpkin shells. Foley squinted, shaded his eyes. When he heard the clattering of the gurney, the crackle of the two-way radio, the anxious voices calling into the front door of the building, he turned and walked slowly out to those who had come to him. He had so many things to tell them.

Foley
Returns

Cousins meant very little in Foley's scheme of things. He remembered his at various ages, at random picnics, as big kids or lanky kids or mean kids, but primarily as just kids. Their air was still filled with the dusty pollen of the Connecticut parks where their parents dragged them on weekends. Even now, it seemed, they sat at the side of the house near the hose spout, listening to the soft *chunk, chunk, chunk* of Foley's aunt—their mother—cutting vegetables for dinner. Their world existed in his mind, he figured, angled and hazy like his memory.

He liked having them suspended like that. Trapped. So Foley hardly listened when his mother told him news of her more successful nieces and nephews—his cousins. They were old now, like him and everybody else. Foley felt sure that he passed thousands of his cousins on the hot, bleached sidewalks of St. Petersburg every day.

One morning, however, as he was drinking coffee in his favorite morning restaurant in Redington Beach, a big glassy place where the sun was kept to a minimum by the angle of the street, he was surprised to read in the national section of the morning paper that his cousin Teddy Napoli had been arrested for shooting and killing a man in Utica, New York. He read the paragraph three times before looking around for someone to show it to. The empty seats of the counter curved off to the cash register. The waitress was busy cutting cheesecake with dental floss, biting her lip in concentration. So he stood, slapped some coins on the counter and left. Outside he folded the paper twice until the story faced out. Standing at the door to his car, with the sun driving its heat off the fender and onto his thigh, he read it again, then again.

He got in, drove for a mile with the vague silence of the air conditioner blowing all over him. Stopped at the rising drawbridge to Treasure Island, he scanned the article once more. He felt sure that this was the same Teddy Napoli. His cousin, his father's sister's second son. Teddy, he knew, still lived in Utica and had always been, his mother assured him, a thug, a tough, and a bartender, the lowest of the low in her book. She rarely mentioned him, if ever. Foley's Aunt Marie claimed she could no longer stand the thought of him. She had forgotten him, she said.

The man in the article was thirty-five, which, Foley knew, was about Teddy's age, and was said to be a bartender who had shot his best customer in an argument over pickled eggs. That was the angle. Humor. There was no picture, but Foley knew that this man who, the article said, turned himself in quietly, was indeed his cousin.

His clearest memory of Teddy involved a childhood trip to Cape Cod. Their two fathers spent the entire vacation bottling small wildlife in formaldehyde, much to the objection of everyone—young Foley, his mother, his Aunt Marie, his brother Hank, his cousin Teddy, and the other, younger cousins. The two fathers had always been driven to find projects on vacations, cleaning the gutters of rented houses or stripping and painting rowboats that didn't belong to them. It mystified the children. "They're happier," Foley's mother told him. "They don't know how to rest."

The families learned not to protest. Still, the smell of the formaldehyde that summer was awful. It overwhelmed the rented cottage's mustiness and the sweet smell of tanning lotions worn by the mothers and children. Foley's Aunt Marie insisted that the two men keep the bottling supplies outdoors, by the side of the house. "I can taste it in the food now," she said one morning, sniffing a forkful of her breakfast. "I can taste it in the pancakes."

They were fierce in their search, bottling everything— small fish, snails, razor clams, sea urchins, baby lobsters, blue crabs, jellyfish, mice—in mason jars that had once held pickles and sauces. Hank laughed about it. One night as they were all driving into town for steamers, he pointed at a dog jogging alongside the road. "Look, Dad," he said, "pickle that."

Foley's father pulled the car to a stop. It was, they all knew, a demonstration of anger, although when he spoke his voice was level. The dog ran up to the door. "That's not funny, Hank," his father said. "Not funny at all."

Foley's uncle swung an arm out and scratched the dog's head. The two families were silent then, although Foley was not sure why. The men were angry, perhaps that was enough. A car honked and passed along the narrow road. Teddy broke the silence. "You're not going to do that to the dog, are you, Dad?"

"No, Teddy," Foley's mother said. "No, baby."

Foley's father started the car up and pulled out. "Good," Teddy said a moment later. "I didn't like what it did to the toad."

None of them had. The toad had been bottled that afternoon. Foley's uncle dropped it in the jar, while Foley's father quickly slapped the lid down. The toad jumped wildly against the lid for a moment and then slowed. It stopped finally, fully stretched, and settled to a delicate balance in midleap. As the toad's head banged against the lid again and again, sending tiny dings out into the kitchen, his uncle laughed loudly, "Ho, ho, now he's going!" Teddy's head pulled back and his mouth slid into a grimace. Foley thought, Teddy's scared. He's wide-eyed.

Foley found himself connecting word and image for the first time. That's what a scared person looks like, Foley knew. He had the sensation that Teddy was not Teddy, that he could be anybody, anybody looking at the one thing that scared everybody. He realized, years later, that at that moment he began to think of his cousins as ideas, rather than people. Teddy became an image of terror. His other cousins fell into place: misery, complaint, fidelity, success, boredom.

His uncle, Foley remembered, once spent the entire afternoon searching out the lower part of the Cape for a large glass jar. Twice he returned to the house, wandered out to the beach where the family had spread and cursed his luck. "Nothing's big enough," he said. "This one won't make it." Yet he would tell no one, except his partner in crime, Foley's father, what it was he planned to bottle in this extra-large jar that he wanted so badly.

Just before dark he returned again, this time carrying a massive jar filled with pickled sausages bobbing in a red brine. The children watched from the living room window as he wobbled the jar, both arms wrapping it tightly, around to the side of the house where the reeds poked up most heavily through the sand. There he unscrewed the lid, dumped the sausages out into a lobster pan, hosed out the jar and refilled it with formaldehyde.

Soon Foley's father joined him. The two of them sat a few yards from the jar, smoking cigarettes and talking quietly as the children watched. "What are they talking about now?" Teddy said, kneeling by the window. "What do they want?" Quite suddenly both fathers stood, stepped on their cigarettes and slid the jar to the side of the porch. The children looked at each other.

"It's under the porch," one of the cousins said softly. "They're going under the porch."

"It's the beehive," Teddy said, looking Foley straight in the face. "They want to do the beehive." He stepped back from the window. "They'll get killed. Bees can kill you!"

All of the children were distinctly aware of the beehive, having avoided that particular side of the house for a week because of it. Teddy was right. His father, Foley's uncle, reached in under the porch, without benefit of any kind of protection, seized the bulbous paper hive by its stem, gave it a yank, wheeled around and plunged it down into the jar. It was a quick, godlike movement and surprisingly few bees escaped the thrust. The two of them stood in the center of the small swarm that did form, without moving. The children noted with reverence that neither of them was stung. "They're not afraid of them," Foley's cousin Lorraine intoned. "They aren't afraid of anything." After a moment the two men screwed the lid back on, bending in the bottom with a pair of rusty pliers so that it could never be reopened. Then they hefted the jar into the house, where they slid it onto the dining room table.

The fascination of the hive, split open and suspended in clear liquid, ended quickly for most of the cousins, who wandered off after a short time, leaving only Foley and Teddy sitting at the dining room table. They turned the sausage bottle periodically for a better view.

"It's like a city," Teddy said, pressing his face against the glass. He stood, walked into the kitchen. "You killed a whole city," he said to his father, who was in the kitchen over his dinner. Foley could hear his uncle eating.

"Go on, Teddy," Foley's Aunt Marie said.

"I bottled it," Foley's uncle said, "so you and everybody else in the family can look at it for the rest of your lives."

"Where do the other bees go?" Teddy asked.

"What other bees?"

"The ones that got away," Teddy said. "The ones that didn't sting you. They don't have anywhere to go now."

"There were no other ones," his father said. "I didn't see any. We got all there were to get."

"They were all around you. They didn't sting you."

"Ha!" his father said. "That's not true. They're all dead."

"You killed them. Except the ones that got out."

"I bottled them," his father said, louder this time. "For you, I bottled them. All of them."

"Why?"

"It's like science," his father said, chewing quickly on a mouthful of cod. "You'll always be able to look at them."

Teddy turned and looked at the beehive. "But I wouldn't want to."

His mother laughed. Foley's mother stood and began clearing. Teddy's father waved him off. "You will, Teddy. You'll want to see things like that. You'll want to remember. I promise."

Teddy's mother went to him and hugged him, lifting him up in her arms. "I hope he forgets," she said to her husband, laughing. She sat and shifted Teddy in her lap until he faced her. She put her hands on his cheeks, shook his head from side to side and said, "Forget, forget, forget."

Foley's father scooped some salt potatoes out of a green ceramic bowl. "Don't listen to her, Teddy. It's your responsibility to remember. It's family."

Foley understood Teddy's dread. The hive was a fierce place, caught just short of saving itself. The hole at the bottom was jammed with bees. The cracks in the sides revealed still more pushing toward the entrance. The liquid had grown amber with the insinuation of honey. All through it bees hung and swirled, mocking flight.

Soon Teddy was shuffled out of the kitchen by his mother and up the back stairs to bed. The adults murmured on in the kitchen. Plates were cleared, coffee served. Foley stayed in the dining room, out of sight, periodically shifting the jar for a new angle on the hive. In the kitchen the parents laughed, and Foley let the bees slow and fall to the bottom of the jar, where they began to gather on their sides. His parents lit their cigarettes one by one from the big wooden matches that caught like flares against the kitchen table. Soon they poured Chianti for one another and later coffee, all the while speaking the strange, silent language of adults.

Three months after the morning he had driven home from Redington Beach to show Grace the article on Teddy, Foley got a letter from him. In it Teddy asked him to come and visit him in prison.

"Dear Dan," the letter began, "I suppose you've heard about my troubles . . ." and was signed "As ever, Ted," which made Foley wonder even more what he had "ever" been to Teddy to make him write to him of all the relatives. Teddy had apologized to Foley for never taking him up on the invitation to visit him in Florida.

Foley could not remember ever having invited Teddy anywhere near Florida, but those invitations went out so frequently and easily to the relatives on both sides of the family that he might well have blurted it out at a wedding or over the phone or even through his mother. Teddy went on to say he had some "minor details" that needed taking care of and would Foley please come up and help him. There was a lawyer's name and directions from the Syracuse airport to the lawyer's office and the prison.

He showed the letter to Grace at breakfast the next morning.

"Jesus," she said, laying the letter on a stack of dry wheat toast. "Who is this guy, anyway?"

"He's my cousin," Foley said.

She glared at him. "I know that. Why is he writing to you now like some immigrant from the old country, asking help? He doesn't even know you."

Foley shrugged, flipped to the box scores. He took a sip of orange juice and a sip of coffee, swished them together and swallowed. Small pleasures.

"When did we ever invite him down here?"

Foley admitted he didn't remember. Nick thumped into the kitchen for some toast before catching the school bus. He wore orange shorts, cut just above the knee and a tank top. His hair fell in a wedge of bangs from the peak of his head onto his forehead. The rest of his hair was cut short, almost shaved. To Foley it seemed that some uncaring person had stripped in only a part of a haircut onto his son's head. But he knew that he missed the point of the haircut and so ignored it. Other things came up.

"Nick," Foley said, "do you ever wear long pants to school?"

Nick snatched the letter up. "Is this the letter from the big house?" Nick looked at Foley, raised his eyebrows. "The joint?"

"It's certainly none of your business, whatever it is," Grace told him. She stood, took the letter from him and handed it to Foley, who thoroughly appreciated the authority of the gesture. "Are you drinking coffee?"

Foley started to answer when he realized that she was talking to Nick. He had yet to get used to this latest habit of his son's. Spreading his fingers on the table, he pushed his hand up and down. This brought to mind push-ups. He made a mental note to run during lunch.

"Black, please," Nick said to Grace. Foley slid him the sports section as he sat.

"What is he talking about when he says minor details?" Grace said, setting Nick's coffee down in front of him.

Nick looked up, his lips slightly parted. "Who?"

Grace ignored him. Foley tried to silence her with a stare. Nick bobbed looks from one to the other. "Who?" he said. "Who?"

"When was the last time you saw him?" Grace said.

"It's been a long time," Foley said. "Years. Ten years."

"Is this the guy in jail?" Nick said, sloshing a glass of orange juice to his lips. "Your cousin?"

Foley leveled a stare. "He's your cousin too." They had discussed this months ago and Nick had had no interest then. His daughter Sophie had suggested that they should write a card to him. Although somehow touched, Foley had squelched that.

Grace stood and turned to the sink. "Are you going?" she asked. "You can't be. You simply can't."

"Where?" Nick said, brushing his hair back from his face. "Prison?"

"Don't be a dullard, Nicholas," Grace said.

Nick rolled his eyes at her. "Come on, Dad. Where are you going?"

"Prison," Foley said and waited to gauge Nick's response. The boy nodded and reached for the cereal box, which disappointed Foley since he felt the word carried some import. *Prison.* Foley wanted to say it again and again. Nick apparently only wanted an answer.

Then Foley said something he'd never said before, and even as he said it, he felt sure he had uttered the wrong words. "He's family."

Grace laughed when he said it. "He's a cousin," she said, cocking a hand on her hip. "One who you haven't seen in thirty years, and he shoots people."

Nick looked up, his cheeks bulging with grains.

"We're your family," Grace said. "Your obligations are here. You don't owe anything to this criminal." Foley started to protest, but Grace went on, waving him off. "I know, I know. He's not guilty of anything yet. But no one is questioning that he shot somebody, are they? With a pistol! That's not my idea of family."

Foley knew what his next step was. "Family is family," he should say, and if Grace kept on, he might shout a little. Even so, afterward he should call the airlines with an abiding resolve and then drive off to the long-term parking, fedora resting level on his head, scowl painted on his face, eyes firmly on the horizon. This is family. He should be ready for anything.

"I've got to go," he said, standing to look Grace in the eyes. "It's the only thing I can do. I don't have a choice. Teddy didn't leave me any."

Grace threw her hands up at that. "Choice!" she said. "Are you serious?"

Foley took a mouthful of coffee and nodded. Grace took a wipe at the counter and said, "You get pushed around so easily. It just makes me sick." Then she reached around behind Foley's back, handed Nick a paper napkin and snatched up her orange juice, which she sipped as she shook her head. "You always have a choice," she said, laying her hand on his wrist.

Foley wished then that Grace had been called upon. She was a better choice, he knew. She could go and be done with it all in a few quick strokes. He remembered how, years before, she could wipe Nick's nose with one hand and turn down the volume on their tiny television with the other. He constantly marveled at her ability to do many things in a single gesture. As if the tasks at hand were a part of one fluid movement.

Foley plodded through things—listing things, checking them off, then rechecking each one. He saw the letter as an appeal, full of expectations that he was someone strong, someone decisive. A problem solver. A protector. A family man. Swift action was called for. Firm decisions. He knew the role. He wanted to play it.

But he had no idea what this kind of family was, this cousin from beyond the edge of the world, from prison. His own words on the matter seemed comic. He was most compelled, he knew, by the tone of the letter—plaintive and brief—and he liked the idea that Teddy felt he could be relied upon. So he had assumed the mantle of family and was beginning to feel its tilt.

He would do what Teddy asked. Teddy needed him, his cousin. Foley would go there as an upstanding man, to help Teddy balance his life, to talk and dig up their childhood. Foley could negotiate, stand up for Teddy, be a symbol of strength, of family ties, someone for Teddy's lawyers to use during the trial.

So, even as Grace fumed, he moved forward—flying off, returning to Utica—leaving everything behind in St. Petersburg, all without knowledge of the promises that compelled him.

As a boy Foley used to joke with his older brother that the city of Utica sat on the axis of the earth's rotation. "It's the vortex of the universe," he would say in another variation of the joke, leaning over the front seat and swirling his hands like a magician for effect, on those Saturdays when his father drove them up from the Saquoit Valley to load the station wagon with supplies for his many business ventures—cases of straws and crates of potatoes for the diner, dusty sacks of fertilizer for his driving range, the mysteriously light cardboard boxes of mortuary supplies for the funeral home.

Hank found the joke hilarious, faithfully laughing each time Foley told it. The whole thing seemed to baffle his father who, Hank insisted, probably wasn't sure what the universe was, let alone a vortex.

"Very funny, Mr. Chatterbox," his father would say. "You're not thinking how much money we're saving by driving into town."

His father was right on that account. Even as a boy, Foley didn't want to think money. The three of them approached the tiny city along roads that paralleled the endless train yards, paved alternately by brick, gravel and cement. When Foley looked at Utica he saw it painted gray every day of the year and then snapped cold every October, until winter ran out in time for the rain to begin again. That wasn't quite the truth, he knew even then, as there were plenty of days when they rolled into Utica, his father's cigar smoke trailing out the window behind them, under blue skies. But to Foley the town seemed cursed in every respect. The beer was local, the baseball team bush league, and movies seemed paler in there than they did in Syracuse or Rochester. His father couldn't understand. Even then Foley was intent on escape.

The question of the vortex of the universe came back to Foley years later as he walked the sidewalks of Utica on his way to see Teddy Napoli, his cousin, the murderer. The wind shot snow in furious circular gusts around his ears. He kept his head down, hands in his pockets. Beneath his feet the sidewalk was broken into blocks, each one of which, without exception, cracked into a network of a thousand dirty veins and each about to be covered by the oncoming snow, the first of the season according to Foley's car rental agent.

"That's the weight of the universe settling here," he said as he walked, carrying on the vortex joke. No one was on the streets to hear him. They were all in tunnels below him, he figured, or bridges above him, avoiding the weather. In fact he could hardly hear himself, which reminded him that he was absolutely alone in this endeavor. No older brother to come along for a drink to fight off the cold before ducking into the county jail, where Teddy was being held before the trial; no wife waiting at the motel with a promise of the search for a good dinner later; no sweet daughter to slip him an apple before he pulled on the heavy glass doors. His mother had refused to come, which hadn't surprised him. It was his mission, he knew. His alone.

He shuffled across the sidewalks until he reached the jail. He went in and, before speaking to anyone, smoked a cigarette in the lobby. He paced to warm himself, with speckled green marble floors under his feet. Each sheet of marble was separated by a thin strip of brass, worn down, he knew, by the shuffling feet of a thousand weary fathers and brothers and wives. All around him there were postings for blood drives.

Finally he dropped his cigarette into a cylindrical ashtray and stepped up to the desk. There were no cops to be seen, at least not for the moment, and Foley stood there staring down at the police blotter, which was absolutely and hopelessly white. He fought off the urge to flip a page back and look for some evidence of crime, of action or complaint. Folding his hands together tightly, he leaned into the office, lifting his heels slightly off the marble floor, and looked toward a heavy white fire door at the back of the office. The door opened quite suddenly and a fat officer with a long unkempt mustache came out laughing.

He straightened upon seeing Foley, jerked the back of his pants by his belt and moved behind the desk. "Can I help you with something?"

"I'm here to see Teddy Napoli," Foley said, easing his heels back down onto the marble. The cop gave him a blank stare, locking his eyes on a point somewhere near Foley's hairline. "He's a prisoner."

"I know who he is," the cop said. "I'm waiting to find out who you are."

"His cousin," Foley said. "Daniel Foley."

The cop took out a ledger and penned Foley's name, mouthing the word "cousin" as he wrote it in under the word RELATIONSHIP. He then flipped the ledger around for Foley to sign and pointed him to a door, which he buzzed.

The fat cop met Foley, who nodded awkwardly, on the other side and led him down a narrow hallway that ran between two collections of felt-lined cubicles. Each one housed its own small machine—the copier, the postal meter, the power stapler.

Foley marveled at the diversity of calendars in each cubicle, and their prominent placement in each space. Rigid-Tool, the American Ferrari Association, Ansel Adams. On some the days were scratched through, while others lagged, pages unflipped, months behind the actual passage of time.

As he had at the blotter, he fought off the urge to reach in and interfere, in this case to synchronize the calendars. He kept his eyes straight ahead on the backside of the big cop, who jingled and swayed from side to side with the weight of gun and keys, his belt perilously strapped in just at the point where his waist fell away most quickly.

Foley felt himself starting to warm up. He slipped off

his jacket as the big cop unlocked a door marked INTERRO-
GATION. In pencil, just under the wire-mesh window, some-
one had written "Give up faith, all you what enter here."
The cop saw Foley looking at the words.

"That's a joke," he said. "Don't pay any attention to
that. I'm supposed to wash that off."

He opened the door for Foley, who stepped into a room
with two stainless steel tables, a set of chairs, a stool and a
window covered with chain-link fencing. "Wait here," the
cop said from the doorway. "Be a minute or two. Someone
will have to stay with you while you talk."

Foley sat and folded his coat over his knees. He read
the desk. "Frank as Pisces" the words said in smooth, loop-
ing Magic Marker letters. Above him the ceiling had hairlike
cracks running out from the light fixture.

The door opened and Foley stood. Teddy came in with
his arms swinging softly at his sides. Foley started to speak,
but the cop, who had followed Teddy in, spoke first.

"Don't touch," he said. "Stay on opposite sides of the
table. If you want coffee, say it now, 'cause I'm not making
two trips." Teddy waved him off and Foley said no thanks.

Teddy looked old. Foley had expected that, but what
surprised him when Teddy walked in the room was that he
could have been anyone. A prisoner. Foley had expected at
least a flicker of recognition, but he never would have picked
Teddy out at a party, or on the street. His hair was long,
still jet black, pulled back in a pony tail, and he had a heavy
beard now.

Foley remembered Teddy as a rail-thin kid, with a crew
cut and no shirt, trailed by the smell of butch wax. This
Teddy, though, this new version of his cousin, was fat and
Foley noticed it most clearly in his cheeks, which were puffy
and round, and his neck, which had creases in it even when
he held his head straight up. He wore standard blue cover-

alls, and had a pink hospital wristband on one arm. To Foley it felt as if they were meeting at the airport. Teddy seemed to view the event as part of some giant hassle.

"Thanks," he said finally. The cop sat and picked up a *People* magazine.

"For what?" Foley said, feeling suddenly defensive. "Coming? Don't thank me. You don't have to."

"Yeah," Teddy said, "but you didn't have to come either." I had no choice, Foley thought. I had to come.

Teddy wheeled around in his seat. "Can I have a cigarette?"

The cop nodded without looking up. Foley reached into his pocket, handed him one, lit it, and then grabbed one for himself. "This is something," Teddy said, spreading his arms, turning his palms up, "isn't it?" He still spat out the first syllables of his words, as if there were some pain involved.

Foley agreed. It was something.

"You're my eighth visitor," Teddy said. Foley wasn't sure what to think of that. Maybe that was a lot.

"You look like your dad now," Teddy said, taking a long drag. "I don't. But you do. Most men do eventually. When was the last time you saw my dad? I don't think I look like him. Do you think so?"

Foley tried to think when the last time he had seen his Uncle Vincent was. They had played golf four years ago. Foley could only remember his shirt that day, which was aqua blue and too small—so that he tugged at it whenever he wasn't shooting. But the only face he could attach to the idea of Teddy's father was an uncle of thirty years ago laughing in his huge way, with Teddy or one of the sisters, sitting in his lap in a large Adirondack chair. He needed a shave. "I suppose so," Foley said. "You look something like him."

There was a long pause in their conversation then,

which Foley, true to the promise he had made to himself on the plane, refused to fill with questions like "How did this happen?" or "How are they treating you?" Teddy probably wanted something big here, and for now maybe it was enough just to be staring into the face of the past.

"I didn't really expect you to come," Teddy said finally. Foley was silent. "Not that you shouldn't have, but you came fast."

Foley shrugged, while his mind mulled over Teddy's doubts. He wasn't sure he wanted to hear them. "Why did you write me?"

Teddy leaned forward and spoke softly. "You want to know the worst thing about being in here?" Foley found himself nodding. "Margarine," Teddy said.

Foley didn't like his role in all this. Here was Teddy, plainly pulling his chain, acting as if the whole thing were a practical joke. He didn't want to hear the punch line to this margarine joke. Better to slap Teddy on the side of the head.

"The bread is dry here, Dan," Teddy said. "So is the corn. You don't get any margarine."

Foley shot a glance at the cop, who didn't seem to be listening. "Why did you write to me, Teddy?"

Teddy leaned back and picked his cigarette up from the ashtray. "I'll tell you, Dan," he said, smiling, "but I want to know why you came."

The question surprised him. He had come here to be told something, not to be asked something.

"Were you afraid of what I might do to you if you didn't come? I mean, after I got out."

"What?" Foley said. This was a threat, plainly.

"Do you think I'm dangerous?"

Foley tried to raise a scowl, but he sensed that he was afraid of something in the room. Teddy was only his cousin. They had spent, at best, several weekends of their life together. He had no idea what to make of that now that they were grown up, each staring at the other as if he were some museum diorama.

"Christ, Teddy. We were kids together. We're cousins."

Teddy nodded. "I figured something like that too. You were a mean kid, but you were reliable."

This vision of himself confused Foley, who perceived himself as neither mean nor reliable, and took both comments as insults coming from Teddy.

Foley decided not to say anything. Teddy slipped a hand into his pocket and pulled out a folded sheet of paper. "I have a list," he said. "There's a lot of things that need doing."

The cop looked up from his magazine. "Don't touch," he said.

Foley took a pen from his pocket. In his wallet he found an automatic teller receipt. "I'll write them down," he said to Teddy. "Go ahead." He drew the number 1 on the back of the slip and circled it.

Teddy unfolded his paper and read. "My dog."

Foley wrote in DOG and then lifted the pen. "What about it?"

"Get rid of her," Teddy said softly.

"Where is she now?"

"I'm not sure. My neighbor's maybe, or my boss's place."

Foley put the pen down now. "Who's your boss? How do I find him?"

"I'll get to that," Teddy said, looking down at the list, as if the next move were Foley's. Foley wrote in SHELTER? next to DOG and penned in a number two below it.

"What else, Teddy?"

The list went on and the entries became more complex. HOUSE—SELL. MOTORCYCLE—SELL. GARAGE—LOCK. BAR—

RETURN. GAS—CUT. PHONE—DISCONNECT. MOTHER—ASK. Each entry prompted a series of questions from Foley, who grew into a sudden familiarity with Teddy's life, with his daily routine, with his different friends and enemies, his onetime plans for the future.

"Is my life insurance policy still good?" Teddy asked at number 8 on the list. Foley didn't know. He was surprised that Teddy had life insurance at all. Strangely—almost absurdly, he thought—the realization pleased him. But when he wrote in INSURANCE—OKAY? he found his hand growing heavy and the back of his neck hot. The list went on, but Foley found himself less aware of Teddy's voice and more aware of his body, the way he lifted his hand to bring the cigarette to his mouth. Foley knew he would be in town a long while taking care of Teddy's business. He would see Teddy again and again. These gestures would become Teddy's, he expected, particular and important to his person. The web of Teddy's life, of his friends, his circumstance, would wind out and out until Foley could see nothing else in here, in this room, in this city. Then just when he reached the point when everything was set, when Teddy's life could teeter forward a little easier, Foley would fly home to his own life, where all of this would grow dim.

"I have some money," Teddy said at number 14 on Foley's list.

"Okay," Foley said without looking up.

"I need you to take it to my lawyer."

Foley looked up and nodded. Teddy smiled, and for a moment he really did look like his father, or like Foley's memory of his Uncle Vinnie gently holding his boy in a sleeping curve.

Now Foley could smell Listerine and cigarette smoke on his breath. "It's at my house. Not a lot, four thousand three hundred and fifty. Cash. Mom's bound to show up there soon or during the trial and I don't want her to find it. Not that it's stolen." He stopped then and reached across to touch Foley's hand. "She'll think it's drug money." He looked at the cop as he spoke. "There was a time when she would have been proud that I'd saved that much. Now it'd just kill her. When something like this happens everything comes untied." Foley nodded.

"I knew you'd come through, Danny," Teddy said, leaning forward. He pushed his chair back suddenly and put his hands flat on his thighs.

"How did you know?" Foley said.

Teddy laughed, then shrugged. "Actually I figured you wouldn't know any better."

"Why didn't you just ask a friend?"

"Get a receipt from that lawyer," Teddy said.

Foley wished then that they had just sent him a card, as Sophie had suggested. He reached in his coat pocket, fingered a photograph he kept there, one of Sophie in a snowsuit, holding a muddy basketball in his mother's back yard. He pulled it out and slid it across to Teddy.

Teddy looked at it and slid it back. "I already have this one," he said. "Your mother sent it to me years ago."

"Why didn't you just ask a friend?" Foley asked again.

Teddy shrugged. "They're lazy," he said. "They wouldn't do what I told them. I figured you would."

"Don't you want me here for the trial?"

"I copped a plea," Teddy said. "No trial."

"What about the lawyers then?" Foley said. "You just want me to pay them?"

"Yup," Teddy said.

"Your letter," Foley said, "I thought you wanted help."

Teddy squinted. "What do you think you're doing?"

"No. With problems, real problems. Family things."

Teddy laughed. "These are things I need doing. That's

what family does. I need a tire, I go to Uncle Al's store and he cuts me a deal."

"That's not what I'm talking about," Foley said. He looked around, as if the answer, the words, might be pinned on the wall somewhere.

Teddy got mad then. "What? You want to be my parole officer?"

"I owe you more than this anyways," Foley said.

"Go to hell," Teddy said. "You don't owe me anything."

Foley leaned back in his chair. "Teddy," he said. "Ted."

"I didn't ask you for money," Teddy said.

"I know."

"I need these things done. You can just do them and go away."

"Look," Foley said, "I just wanted . . ."

"You wanted to fix everything up," Teddy said. "Well, you can't. So just forget about that. This is a done deal."

Foley could see that now. "You want directions to my house?" Teddy asked. "Or do you figure you should know your way there just because you're family? Maybe you can just sense your way there." Foley said nothing, picked up the pen and motioned for him to finish, to begin again, to leave him be.

The house was a good ways north of Utica. The money was hidden in the tool shed, in a coffee can. When the directions were straightened out, Teddy stopped talking and motioned for another cigarette. Foley gave him one and lit it. "You know I have a picture of the two of us on Lake Michigan, when you taught me to swim," Teddy said. "Christ, you were skinny."

Foley remembered that quite suddenly: buoying Teddy's chest with his fists, the murky bottom below. Teddy had been so easy to hold up that they went at it for hours.

"Do me one more favor, would you, Dan?" Teddy said before he stood. "Give the house a once-over, would you? It's a mess. My mom would die."

Foley found himself nodding and standing. He shook Teddy's hand. "Is that it?" he asked as the cop laid a hand on Teddy's arm.

"That's plenty, Dan," Teddy said, before he turned to the door. "I wouldn't ask just anyone."

The disappointment had been slow in coming on. He had left the jail feeling relieved actually. Teddy wanted a favor. No problem. People wanted favors all the time. But his last vision, of Teddy being led out of the room by the fat cop, stuck with him.

He had expected the hard part to be over when he finished the list, when he scratched in the last number. He drove the long roads, humped as they were from years of careless repaving, out to Teddy's home, a white house on a small rise. If Teddy had asked for money, Foley would have gladly obliged (despite the limit he and Grace had agreed upon before he left). If Teddy had asked him to take care of his mother, or an illegitimate child even, Foley felt sure he could have managed it.

Foley had been sent out on errands. He would start at the bottom of the list, as he always did, and cross each number out with a single line. He did this every day, it seemed, in the office and at home, for his children, for his friends. Teddy had asked for nothing. Maybe he had read Foley just right.

This was Foley's cousin, once a little boy—the wearer, Foley remembered (again suddenly), of many-colored crowns, fashioned from the cardboard furtively pulled from his father's dry cleaning. This was his cousin, the one who, everybody in the family knew, loved Heath Bars. Hadn't Foley himself given him twenty on his tenth birthday? He had, and Teddy had loved him for it! And Foley, upon remembering this, suddenly saw his cousin pale and sad, and missing all the things Foley had forgotten about.

The house, which Foley found just as the sun broke through the heavy skies, was set back from the road at the end of a long muddy driveway. Large rocks, slashed with bands of orange paint to guide the nighttime driver, lined the edges of the driveway. It seemed a strangely thoughtful thing for Teddy to have done. But as he made his way up to the house, Foley began to see, between the stones, the detritus of a lifetime. Mufflers. Cigar boxes, warped and softened by the rain. Bicycle wheels. Bags of aluminum cans. He found himself admiring the disorder, believing for a moment that each item or pile might have just been set down in some as yet unseen pattern. In fact, despite the decay, he could see how Teddy had done just that. He had left these things there, without considering the possibility of a long absence from it all, without thinking about the elements or the way time might wear each thing down. This was his life, from which he had been taken without warning. The whole scene was like some artifact, some testament to the fluidity of his existence, carelessly left for Foley to bear witness to.

He parked next to the house and walked across the frozen ground, past a gutted Buick, to the shed attached to the far side of the garage. He pushed on the door. The shed smelled like damp canvas. Foley hit the light switch, which didn't work. Still, there were slats of light that poured in from the edges and nooks of the shed.

The dirt floor was covered with machine parts, pulled apparently from the heart of a giant mechanical horse, the kind a child would ride at a supermarket or a fair, that lay on its side on a pile of kindling. Teddy's tools were spread so randomly, so honestly, across the dirt floor that Foley felt Teddy might have just gone out for a cigarette. He nudged a ratchet coupling with his toe. On the far wall there were several cans and jars, just as Teddy had said. He walked to the wall and bent over to retrieve the can. It was there to be sure, just behind a large jar that sat close to the outside wall. A shaft of light poked through a missing plank, falling across the dusty back of the jar.

It was the beehive, hanging in brown liquid, the edge of its frayed paper hide peeled out, moving softly like a leaf of kelp. Foley lifted the jar with both hands and set it on a bench above the mechanical horse. The bees, several hundred now, continued to gather in the bottom as they had on the afternoon of their capture thirty years before, although they were blacker now, smaller than Foley remembered. He dusted the jar off and examined the hive, which had split and gone soft over the years. It rolled and changed shape slightly, like a loaf of bread suspended just below the surface of a pond. Its hide was still full, as with each turn still more bees came forward and twirled free.

Foley reached down and got the money, folded it into a big lump and threw the can down in the oily innards of the mechanical horse. He slipped the money into his coat pocket and wrapped his arms around the old sausage jar.

What would he do with it? He might carry it home with him on the plane, show it to his children, take measure of their reaction. "This is something that has always been. This is just as it was then," he wanted to say. "This is me." But none of that was true. Now the hive was like a found object, a bone or a shard of pottery. Once it had been something on its own terms—at best a living place, a captured energy, at worst a science project. He knew that it had been part of something larger too—his family—and that was why Teddy had hung on to it. But now, by itself, forgotten in the back of a toolshed, it was nothing. And he could see then that his family, with all of its old routes of comfort, with its convincing balance, its soothing geography, wasn't there anymore.

So, on his way back to town, after cleaning Teddy's filthy kitchen and picking up the yard, Foley stopped by the side of the highway and rolled the hive out of the back seat of his rented car, down an embankment. There he watched it shatter and transform itself into something new, something that would decay and disintegrate in a few months, a thing you might step over without taking notice. Then he got back behind the wheel, grasped it and spoke, reminding himself out loud of promises still unkept.

Foley's Motto

F oley took mottos. Pithy things like "Dare to be im-
perfect" and "Always take the stairs." He changed
them every few days, adopting suggestions freely.
When people—the janitor in his office building, for instance—asked after his motto for the day, he took pleasure
in telling it to them. It made him feel like he had a plan.

He found that the more absurd mottos, often ones made
up on a whim, were easier to live by. For instance, when his
motto was "If it's not orange, I won't drink it," he lived for
weeks drinking only juice and soda. No one seemed to mind.
Word spread. It got laughs. But when he started in with
three simpler mottos—"Love something," "Finish something" and "Expect nothing"—he got into trouble. That finished him on mottos altogether.

These simpler mottos were stolen from the office of Max
Webber. Foley was having a mole taken off his back when
he noticed a cut of cypress trunk above a clock on the wall.

It was a heavily varnished piece of wood, with the words LOVE SOMETHING decoupaged across it.

"That's new," Foley said, after Max had deadened the mole. Max had scissors in his hand. "Jesus, Max," Foley said over his shoulder, "Can't you burn it off or something?"

Max slipped his glasses down his nose. "You want a scar?"

Foley shook his head, let Max work. "I like that," he said. "Love something." Max snipped. "What does that mean?" Foley asked as Max put a piece of gauze to the bleeding. "Love anything?"

Max shrugged behind him and began cauterizing. "Love your job, I guess. It's zen. I bought a bunch of those things from a kid in a parking lot in Kissimmee."

The cauterizer popped and crackled and Foley gritted his teeth. "I can feel that."

"Only a little," Max said softly.

"I'm going to use your sign," Foley said. "I'm going to take it for a motto."

"Sit up," Max said. He looked at the sign and laughed. "You can have it. I've got more. You can have them all." He put a tiny bandage on Foley's back. "Don't scratch."

"Love something," Foley said. "That's my new motto."

Max turned from him, wrote in his file. "Just don't scratch," he said.

As a boy his motto had been "A Foley never makes two trips." It was something he and Hank developed while unloading the groceries from his father's Buick. "One trip at all costs," Hank always said as he piled bag upon bag— potatoes upon bread, pickles upon flour—in young Foley's arms. Once loaded, the two of them made a mad rush for the back steps. If a carton of eggs was lost on the trip to the kitchen, Hank called it a necessary sacrifice. When their

mother protested, they laughed her off and recited their
motto. The pleasure lay in the repetition of the phrase. Foley
pretended that it implied character, perseverance, and he enjoyed saying it word for word with his brother each time
they opened the trunk of the car.

Years later Foley's twelve-year-old son Nick latched on
to this same motto. He repeated it with relish and begged
his father to load him down whenever they took the groceries in together. "A Foley never makes two trips," he'd
say. "Foley pride." It led to many disasters, especially when
he attempted the feat by himself. Grace complained. "I can't
buy anything in bottles," she said. "I have to carry the eggs
in my purse."

Outwardly Foley discouraged Nick, but he often found
himself at the back of the car loading the boy down. He
admired Nick's dedication and enjoyed sharing the task with
him when he could. The sharp tops of the grocery bags
in his face made him giddy for his own boyhood. He saw
nothing wrong with losing the occasional half gallon of
Cranapple.

Nick loved all of Foley's mottos, for that matter. Often
they occurred to Foley at the breakfast table and he made a
habit out of scrawling them on paper napkins, which he
taped to the side of the butcher's block for Nick to find
hours later. Nick pinned the notes to the back of his bedroom door like a collage. "You ought to make a calendar
out of these things," he told Foley once. "They're like fortune cookies." Foley liked the sentiment.

When Foley told him that his new motto was "Love
something," Nick couldn't see the point.

"Don't you mean love somebody?" he said.

Foley shook his head. "Love something."

"It's too easy," Nick said. "You could pick anything.
You could love a toaster." He laughed. "Love a toaster."

Foley was stung. Nick had always encouraged loyalty

to the mottos. He had cheered Foley on, demanding that he live by his words. Now he was making fun.

"Not just anything," Foley said. "Something. Maybe something new. Like woodworking. Maybe I'll decide to love baseball the way you do."

"You don't know anything about it," Nick said. "How can you love it?"

"I'll learn," Foley said. "I want to. You can teach me." At that, Nick shrugged and Foley went for the sports section.

Foley soon discovered that his son understood baseball in a deep, almost animal way. Foley could not keep up. Nick talked baseball to his barber. With only the slightest invitation, he could effortlessly draw up arcana and obscure statistics about any ballplayer. Foley could point to any infield during any Saturday afternoon game and Nick would know something about everyone playing. Foley always asked about the third baseman, hoping to stump him. "He used to sing in a band," Nick would say. Or "He hasn't hit a lick since he found Jesus."

Foley wanted to be able to talk about the game with some authority, to share this with Nick, so at Nick's suggestion, he took to reading the box scores. There were patterns there, Nick told him, things to latch on to. Foley began to assemble tiny notebooks to help him discern hitting trends, strikeout-to-walk ratios. Every morning, he took fifteen minutes poring over the box scores, working to get all the numbers down. Only after he finished his daily entries in the notebooks did he stop to look over the game summaries, the standings. But the particulars of the pennant race hardly interested him. He got himself hooked on watching the performances of the lesser knowns—the scrubs, Nick called them. He began to get up early and he chafed when the morning paper was late.

Nick thought the whole thing was a howl. "Dad, just check the stats every Sunday," he said. "The numbers are more accurate." Foley felt that Nick missed the point. The daily charting was important. The notebooks were the thing. "I'm trying to learn something," Foley told him. "I want to outstrip the experts."

About a year later the truth came out. As they hefted plasterboard up the back stairs to the attic, which they were remodeling, Nick asked, "What if I threw your baseball notebooks out?" They cranked the board around the turn to the second flight.

"Lift," Foley said. "I'd just start them again. It's okay. Down," he instructed. "Throw them out if you want. I already know the patterns."

Nick hooted at that. And it was a lie. Foley was bluffing. The books made no sense even to him and he didn't like watching the game. Truth was, he had quit keeping the books. He was about to give up on baseball.

"I simply picked the wrong thing to love," he told Max one afternoon on the golf course. Max had dragged him into playing in a Wednesday night league. They were a team, matched each week with another twosome. Foley played out of Max's bag. He had a soft touch with the short irons.

Max shrugged. "Wrong motto," he said as he stepped down into a sand trap.

Foley argued that. "I've never had a motto that didn't work. 'Love something' is good."

Max indulged Foley on the subject of his mottos these days. No one else ever asked about them anymore. Foley had stuck with "Love something" for over a year now. His janitor had been disappointed from the start. "That's soft, man," he had said when Foley told him. "That's cheese."

Max stood on his tiptoes and eyed the pin. "So pick another motto," he said. "Is that downhill?"

Foley folded his arms. "Down and to the right."

Max punched his shot off the lip of the trap and left it short of the pin. The two other members of the foursome said "Nice out" in unison, then began rumbling around in their bags. They were mailmen. Max watched the ball settle on the far side of the green, then turned to Foley. "I have other signs in my office. You could pick another one."

"Name one," Foley said.

"The sign in the lab says 'Finish something.' That's a good one for you."

Given how easily he had let baseball slip away, Foley had to agree. "Finish something," he said, nodding. "Okay. I can stick with that." He felt the old enthusiasm growing then. He wanted to quit the golf game, run home and tell Nick. Instead he caught himself, decided to really pick the right thing this time. Something he could finish. He gave it a great deal of thought as he watched the mailmen take their hacks.

At dinner that very night, Foley announced his new motto. Grace showed little interest. "I want to try to build a long boat," he told her. "A big one. One with sixteen seats. Or eight at least."

"What are you going to make it out of?" Grace asked.

Sophie had made the lentil soup. She was watching closely to see that everyone ate with gusto. Nick half stood, reached across the table for the salt, then clumped back down. "There's plenty of salt in the soup, Nick," Sophie said.

"Rock maple," Foley said. "Or bird's-eye maple. I don't know. Hardwoods."

Grace plainly hated the idea. She wanted to know where he was going to build it, where he was going to get the hardwoods he said he needed.

"The city," he said, meaning Tampa. "I'll rent a place, and I know people who have maple. I'll be able to find it." Grace shook her head. The children didn't seem to hear.

He worked on the boat for a year—in his garage it turned out—then changed the project in midstride to an Adirondack guide boat, a four-seater. Eventually it became a sailboat after he designed a mast and rigging system. The boat never hit the water, but Foley never declared the project dead. It sat, half built, on a pair of sawhorses in one bay of his garage. Anyone who saw it there might assume that it was still creeping toward creation.

Grace couldn't stand his aborted efforts. "All these skeletons! All this wasted effort!" she shouted one afternoon, standing over his unfinished garden. "We've been working on this for years. We'll never be done!"

"I can do this," he said, pressing his hand in the wet dirt. "I can finish this in an afternoon." He had started the garden three years ago. Inside the house, lying flat and dusty on the ends of his shelves, he had several books on perennial flowers and English gardens. They had done him no good. He lived in Florida. The soil was sandy, full of tiny shells. He grew only vegetables in the far end of the garden.

"You couldn't finish that in a lifetime," Grace said. She was being mean. Things were rocky between them. Tense. Earlier, she had come outside to explain the taxes to him and found him sleeping in the hammock. When he showed no interest in the taxes, she began pointing out the remains of his projects; he made an effort to get to work then. That's when he got down on his knees.

"You can't finish anything," she said, throwing her hands in the air. She became theatrical. He liked it. "Bring me something finished! Show me one thing!"

"I've finished plenty of things," he said. He stood then and looked around. There was no immediate evidence to lean on. He had taken the day off to scrape the house. At midmorning he took a break and got started cleaning the garage. At noon he stopped for the nap.

"Everything around here is three-quarters done!" Grace shouted. "I'm sick of it! Our whole life is three-quarters!"

"Grace, I work," Foley said. "If I had a little time, I could knock this off in a day or two. I could finish this."

"Finish this!" Grace said, flipping him the taxes. Pages tumbled out of the folder and spread at his feet.

Foley tried to laugh. "I'll have it by dinner."

He didn't, though. The taxes had always baffled him and when he tried to sort through the papers, after setting up a desk of sorts out in the garage, he grew more and more frustrated. Finally he left the folder in the bottom of the longboat/sailboat. At dinner, when Grace shook her head, he shrugged and ate his zucchini.

His zucchini! Grown in the south end of his garden! He speared one of the slices and held it up on the end of his fork. "This," he said, "is something I grew. It's finished." He put the zucchini in his mouth and chewed. Nick laughed.

"You planted it," Grace said. "I watered it and watched it grow."

"I picked it," Foley said, looking down at the zucchini as if it were really his, as if he owned each piece.

"You picked it when I told you to," Grace said. "Otherwise it would have died out there with your tomatoes."

"My tomatoes!" Foley said. In April, he had planted

them in buckets of cow manure as his father always had. He vaguely remembered staking them early in the summer.

"Rotten on the vine," Grace said. Nick reached for the bowl of pasta. Then Grace held up a slice of zucchini, just as Foley had, with the same sense of ceremony. "I cut these. I cooked them. I finished them." She opened her mouth wide, bit down on the zucchini and chewed.

"What's going on here?" Sophie asked, plainly puzzled.

"Your father never finishes anything," Grace said.

Sophie shrugged. Nick glanced at Foley and back at Grace. He nodded. "What does that mean?" Foley asked. "Do you agree?"

"I don't know," Nick said. He took a forkful of pasta and considered things. "I guess so." At that, Grace tilted her head and stared at Foley from the other end of the table. Apparently she considered that a victory.

That was how he became interested in bringing her something. Something finished. He made a list of the things he had finished. He thought he might present the list to Grace, like a letter or a poem. This is how the list began: "I am an architect, I have finished many things."

As he drove back and forth from his house on the Gulf, east across the top of St. Petersburg and over the bay to Tampa, where he had an office, he dwelled on the things he had finished. He kept a mental list all day and added it to the master list when he returned home each night. Soon this list curled down two sheets of legal paper.

He listed the houses he had designed. The bank on Treasure Island. The yogurt kiosk at the mall in Clearwater. The bookstore in Ybor City. His mother's new garage. Their very own attic.

One morning, long after he had quit baseball and weeks

after he had finished the list, he walked into the kitchen and found Grace mashing eggshells in a ceramic bowl. He stood next to her, with his arm touching hers, and looked down into the bowl. Grace was clearly trying for uniformity here. She wanted the pieces small. He thought she looked very beautiful mashing eggshells and he said so.

"Compost," Grace said, giving the bowl a turn, not looking up, throwing in one last mash. "Calcium."

Foley squinted, said nothing.

Grace turned with the bowl and emptied the eggshells into a paper bag at her feet. Before she folded it shut, Foley caught a glimpse of rotting fruit. "It's for the compost heap," Grace said. "I have now taken over the compost heap."

Foley nodded. He had forgotten about that. He was not sorry to lose control of it, but he reached for the bag. "I'll take care of it," he said.

Grace brushed his hand away, snatched the bag from him. "No," she said. "I'll do it."

Foley could hear her anger. "I don't mind. It's my garden," he said. "And I started the compost heap. I'm the one who got us into this."

Grace's chin dropped. "Your garden!" She brushed past him quickly and kicked the back door open. Foley watched her walk out into the center of the lawn. She looked like she was marching, as if someone were keeping a beat for her. When she stopped suddenly, he found himself in the doorway. She turned. "It's not your damned garden. It's mine," she shouted. "It's my garden!"

"I started it three years ago," Foley said. "I've been working on it."

That made Grace madder. "You mow the lawn!" she said sarcastically. "You rake!"

"Right!" Foley said. He thought for a moment that she was agreeing with him.

She shook her head when he said that. The bag of compost dangled from the fingers of her left hand. "You spent one Saturday on it three years ago and you think it's yours? You mow the lawn and you think everything's done?"

"Are you going to start on this finishing thing again?" Foley said.

"I'm sick of your projects," she said softly. He could barely hear her.

"Because if you are," he went on, "I have to tell you that I have a list now. A list of all the things I've finished."

Grace tilted her head and squinted. "What?"

"I have a list," Foley said again. "I can show you."

"A list!" Grace shouted. Foley walked to her, putting his hands out, figuring on calming her. He had hoped the list might interest her. "A list!" she shouted again. "I've got a list for you! A list of all the shit you've left me with!" He could almost touch her now. "Shhh," he said, not so much because their shouting was attracting attention as because this had always calmed her before. Her face grew tight with what Foley knew was disbelief. When he got a hand on her and tried to pull her close, she reached back and hit him in the side of the head with the bag of compost. She caught him hard, on the neck. It felt wet and sharp. He went to his knees.

It hurt, but Foley was surprised more than anything else. He put his hands to his neck and pushed his face down into the grass, a gesture meant to show pain. He hoped that Grace would be surprised too and sorry, but after he lay there for a while, in the grass and the banana peels and the mush, it soon became clear that she was gone, that she had walked away without laying a hand of comfort on him, without issuing a single apology. For a while he stayed put, silent, face down, hoping she would see him from the house and think she had knocked him out. Soon he heard the car start. Then he heard the flies.

★   ★   ★

Not long before Grace asked him to leave, Foley finally read her his list. He later realized that it was the last straw, but at the time he saw the list as an accomplishment in itself.

They were in bed. She wanted no part of it and rolled over, cocooning the blanket around her. Foley read anyway. Grace lay still and he assumed she was listening. Just as Foley finished the section outlining all the buildings, all the offices and motels, all the storefronts and fascias he had designed, Grace responded. She still didn't move; she said, "You started them. Somebody else finished them."

"I finished the designs," he said, ruffling the paper. He was only halfway down the list.

Grace laughed. "That's just it," she said. "Plans."

"I finished the attic," he said. "I did that by myself. Mostly."

Then Grace said, "Wall sockets." Foley understood the reference. He had left holes in the plasterboard for wall sockets that were never installed. "Corner bead," Grace said. She had been after him to get the last bit of spackling done. It had been a year. "Risers," she said softly. She was right. The stairs were unfinished.

Her list went on too. Her voice never wavered and she never paused once. Soon Foley started in again with his list and they went back and forth, like a campfire song.

"Paid off the car."

"Unvented dryer."

"Pulled up the carpet in the living room."

"Ungrouted tiles."

That sort of thing. Foley stayed with her, item for item, until his list was finished. Grace was still going strong. Angrily he continued, pulling what he could remember from the last few days and weeks. Grace was calm about it—and brutal, he thought—though she never once rolled over or even stirred. He watched her breathing as they argued. The slope of her back rose and fell at even intervals. When he finally could come up with nothing else, she was silent. "You make it sound like our house is falling apart," he said, resting a hand on her shoulder. "You make it sound like our life is such a mess."

"Yes," she said firmly, as if the word itself was another item from the list, another ragged edge of the life he had set up for them.

After Grace asked Foley to leave, he moved in with Max Webber for a while. Max was a widower. He liked to stay up late for the West Coast baseball scores. He ate grilled cheese sandwiches and lite beer and just about nothing else for dinner. Foley adapted. He did so without the use of mottos.

Grace stayed in touch. She called him two or three times a week. "I hope you're not falling into some rut," she'd say. "How much television are you watching?" Foley found it touching that she was concerned about him. He went back and forth from being angry with her, to being hungry for her company. To his mind, they had been pulled apart by something nameless, something that was eating Grace up from within, a force he couldn't understand. In the weeks before he'd left, Foley had asked her straight out: "Why should I leave?"

"Because you drive me crazy."

"Why?" he'd ask again.

Here Grace's answers were always slightly different. "It's so simple," she said one afternoon, on the patio. "You can't accept anything about the world, but you never change anything." Another time, as she washed the car: "With you everything is watching, watching, watching. It's like living with a golden retriever." Once, as he helped her on with a coat: "It's your lying." Then, after she had asked for the separation, after the paperwork was begun: "I want to finish this house. I want to get on with things. You. You don't seem to want at all."

To Foley these responses seemed disconnected. It was as if she had to make up new reasons each time they fought. He knew that she was trying to give him a picture of himself, but he couldn't focus. He felt connected to the family in a way Grace didn't seem able to grasp.

When he brought up the children, Grace said, "These kids will survive. They have balance. Besides, no one's asking you to desert us. Just leave me alone is all."

"I want to be a guardian for my children," he said. "I want to help them."

Grace laughed. "They're the ones who'll do the helping. Besides, you can still be there for them."

"I want to protect them," he said. "They're children."

"There's no way to protect them from everything." Grace shook her head. "Learn to protect yourself first."

For a while Foley mulled that as a motto: "Protect yourself." But it seemed too singular, too selfish. Besides, his family was falling apart, or he was falling out of it. Mottos were pointless now. Advice came from all sides—from friends, fellow workers, waitresses, in-laws, from Max, even from Sophie and Nick. Mottos seemed to be just another piece of advice, valueless in the abstract, troublesome when acted upon. He quit listening, even to himself.

Work was difficult. He'd risen to partner in his firm, but he now hated everything about his life there—the slant of light through the windows, the piles of slick catalogues along the walls of his office, the samples of wall sconces and ceiling tiles that filled his storeroom. He hated the levity of office interchange, the chipper look in his secretary's eye. When people asked after his motto now, he whirled from them and threw up his hands, so that they might see he was dangerous, electric, disconnected.

When it became too much—all of it, his life with Max, visiting his own children on weekends, in malls which he had designed, watching Grace from a distance as she brought his household projects to a close—he decided to leave St. Petersburg for a while. He took his profit sharing, said good-bye to his partnership and took a job in Tallahassee. It seemed a clean break. His janitor agreed. "This whole thing reeks of a fresh start," he said as he helped Foley pack his office into liquor boxes.

"I'll be back and forth," he told Nick and Sophie. They took the news stoically, on the couch in the living room. Foley felt that they were regarding him suspiciously, as if he were a substitute teacher. It made him feel foreign and old, as if the floor under his feet was rotten, weak.

Before he left he returned to get some furniture from Grace. She helped him tie a chair to the roof of his car. "You're on your own now," she said. "It's the ultimate Foley adventure." He gave her a kiss and took Nick to help him move.

On the way up the bleached highway to Tallahassee, Nick asked Foley whatever had become of his mottos. Foley explained about the ones he had taken from Max's signs and how they had failed him.

"Yeah," Nick said, leaning his head against the window. "I like those signs too."

"They're simple," Foley said. "They should be easy to live by."

"You didn't pick the best sign, though," Nick said.

Foley shot a glance at him. "What?"

"Dr. Webber's best sign is 'Expect nothing.' It's in the waiting room."

Foley nodded. "That's a good one."

"I know," Nick said. "I think that's from a war movie or something."

"Expect nothing," Foley said. He was trying it out.

They had driven on for about a hundred miles when Nick, who had been sleeping, woke suddenly and asked, "So, is that your motto now?"

"What?" Foley said. "Expect nothing?"

"You need one," Nick said. "I think you did better when you had mottos."

Foley took Nick's advice. He was going off into the distance, over the curve of the earth it seemed. Once again he needed something to guide him.

After he set up his life in Tallahassee, Foley made return visits to St. Petersburg regularly. He learned to enjoy the drive. He traveled Route 19, the two-lane highway, which ran closer to the Gulf than the interstate, and listened to the talk radio.

He went down on weekends and stayed in the house with Grace and the kids. Sophie wanted his advice on colleges, so he began to come more often. He still played golf with Max when he could, though Max was more and more into tarpon fishing now. Life began to seem more like it used to, except for the long drive that sliced up each end of his week.

There came a time when Foley began to congratulate himself. He was rolling with the punches, rescuing his life. He began to give credit to his motto, "Expect nothing."

When he told it to a secretary in his new office, she brought him a wooden plaque the next day with the motto burned into it. Foley offered to pay her for it, but the secretary said no. "My husband liked your motto," she said. "He wants to make more of those, if you don't mind. He thinks they'll really sell." Foley said he didn't mind at all.

One night on the trip down Route 19, the moon was full and the road seemed to have reversed itself. In the moonlight, the pavement appeared to be white, the traffic lines black. It was a new effect for Foley, who wished that Nick and Sophie could see it. For a long stretch of road, there didn't seem to be any other cars. He marveled at how incredibly straight the highway was. Then he began to play, taking his hands off the steering wheel, turning off the lights, and finding, to his amazement, that he kept on in his lane. Next he began to look in the rearview mirror for long periods of time, watching closely the road that pulled away from him. Then, driving without the lights again, he watched the road ahead for any sign of life, a streetlamp, a gas station, another car. It brought to mind keeping watch for a lighthouse.

He stopped the car eventually, to get a closer look at the effect of the moon on the pavement. The road was bone white, lined by inky forests of scrub pine. He looked off down the road for another car. None came.

All of this spooked him. He slid back in, turned the key and switched on the lights. Up ahead there was a tiny flicker, like the reflector of a bicycle. He couldn't see much, so he flashed his brights. For a moment it appeared to be a large cat, but he squinted and saw that it was an owl, sitting on a fencepost near the shoulder of the road. Foley turned off the engine, leaving the lights on, keeping the owl directly in the light.

It was brown, about a foot tall, and plainly frozen by the high beams. It had yellow eyes. He had seen deer frozen like this as a boy, but what struck him now was how much the whole scene looked like a textbook illustration. Nothing moved, yet everything suggested movement.

He wanted a closer look, so he got out. He found himself speaking to the owl as he approached. "Hello, Mr. Owl," he said. "Hello."

Foley stood not more than four feet from it for more than a minute. A truck came up from the opposite direction and he figured that would break the owl's trance, so he backed off. The truck roared by; the owl remained fixed. Foley stepped closer.

"Hey!" he shouted. "Go to hell!" He waved his arms in the air, then jumped up and down in front of the headlights. Then, suddenly possessed by the notion that the owl was actually dead, he walked straight up to it and poked it with his finger. It spread its wings, and Foley ducked, but the owl didn't take its eyes off the headlights.

Foley walked back to the car and silently took inventory of what he had here. This was something marvelous; something he could tell stories about. But he wanted more; he wanted his wife, his children to see this. He had visions of capturing it now, of releasing it with them in his garden. Perhaps it would nest there. Surely Grace would love that.

Opening the back door of the car, he knew that he would bring it to them. He could already hear their questions, their astonishment. In the back seat there were several grocery sacks full of clothes that needed washing. He emptied them onto the floor, then slipped one bag into another, then another into another, until they were four thick. He slipped a pillow case over the outside of that. Then, punching the inside of this collection of bags—this new, stronger bag—to check it, he decided that it would do.

He ran up to the owl this time, half thinking it might fly away. It was almost crouching, its head slightly turned toward the car. It seemed to see something in the light. Foley then turned to look into the light for himself. It made him feel naked and stupid.

He shielded his eyes, looked away. After figuring several ways to slip the bag over the owl, he finally decided to come up behind it and drop the bag down swiftly. He did so and to his surprise the owl was still. He gently squeezed the bottom of the bag shut and lifted.

With the owl in the bag, he moved quickly back to the car. The feeling was much the same as holding a baby for the first time—so light, so surprising. He turned the bag sideways, folded it closed and set it carefully on top of the clothes that lay in the back seat. He had still heard nothing from the owl; it hadn't moved yet that he could tell.

When he started the car, Foley let out a whoop. He had found something. It had been easy. His family would love it. "I stopped the car and there it was," he heard himself telling them. "This was not something I was looking for." Nick might say Foley's motto then—"Expect nothing!"— for all of them to hear, or they might all say it together. It could be a way of life.

Ten minutes after he started driving again, Foley heard a scrabbling sound in the back seat, the sound of talons on grocery sack. He slowed the car a little, in preparation to take a quick look, and the owl exploded up out of the back seat, flapping and tearing at everything. "Jesus!" Foley shouted. "Jesus!" And at that the owl was on him, driving its beak into his scalp, pulling back on his hair, and again and again. He brought his arms up, let go of the wheel, and slammed on the brake. The bird's wings beat all around him and he could feel the soft parts of his face being torn. When the car jammed to a stop against a bridge abutment, Foley had a fleeting thought that the bird might stop, that it might know he was beaten. Instead it flipped around to the back of his head and got a talon into his ear. Foley found himself shouting, reaching for the door and swatting for the bird all at once. "Stop!" he yelled and the bird dug into his other ear. He began to shake his head violently and then, suddenly, the bird fell over into the back seat. Foley hooked a finger in the door handle and slipped out onto the pavement.

He was a mess and he lay there on the pavement feeling like he might as well die, that was how bad things were. He listened for the sound of oncoming cars, watching for their lights. Soon he could feel the cool pavement and the burning of his ears. He would live, it seemed; so he rolled over, then stood.

He had no idea if the owl was still in the car. The dome light was out, apparently from the battle. He walked around the car and gingerly opened the doors. There was blood all over the inside of the windows. He touched himself. His shirt was soaked. He began to check himself. His nose was cut badly and his ears felt numb. His face was slick with blood.

The car was wedged up against the edge of the bridge, one wheel off the ground. Foley sat down on the guard rail nearby. Soon a truck drew up, flashed its lights and slowed. Foley kept his head down. The truck hissed to a stop. When he looked up it seemed to be the middle of the day, the truck's headlights had lit everything to a smoky blue. In front of Foley stood the truck driver—a tall black man, wearing blue jeans and boots. Something rattled when he walked.

"Good, kind Christ," the man said. "Who did this to you?"

Foley could think of nothing except the owl. "Do I look bad?"

"Looks like you need a new ear," the man said, kneeling. "You're bleeding." Foley could smell tomatoes.

"An owl," Foley said. "There's an owl in my car."

"What are you talking about, man?" the truck driver said. "Wait a minute, let me call someone." He jogged to the truck.

Foley could hear only snippets of what the truck driver said on the radio—man, blood, bridge. Things like that. But Foley had an idea that somehow the man had gotten through to Grace and Nick and Sophie, that maybe they could come to get him. That cheered him. Or maybe they would be there anyway, in the ambulance, or waiting at the hospital.

When his family was gathered around him, they would chide him for not taking more care and warn him not to stop his car late at night. They would all laugh about the owl, Foley felt sure. He would shake his head, express wonder at what he'd brought upon himself.

As he recovered they would do kind things for him— bring him magazines and wet washcloths. He'd thank them again and again. When he was nearly recovered—resting in a lawn chair, letting the sun heal his wounds—they would be kind when they asked him why. Why did you stop that night? Why did you leave us? Why did you return?

That's when Foley would say "I don't know. I didn't know." Those were the words he lived by.

Foley,
Avenger

A long time ago, in St. Petersburg, I ordered my lawn clippings by the curb in neat piles. The lizards kept to either side of the drying grass, the curling palm fronds, the random pickings, the refuse from my gutters. Still, the piles crawled with life: millipedes and roaches, tiny worms. The Gulf was a block away. The beaches, where I often took long walks, teemed with crabs at night; a fist in the wet sand pulled up coquinas and transparent animals, mites and small mollusks, that quickly slipped away. My neighbors all fished the surf. Successfully.

When I moved away from the Gulf, to Tallahassee, I failed to notice the life at my feet. I felt muffled. The Gulf was far away. Heat collapsed on the city. I ignored the lawn. I hired a yard man and began to live indoors.

My daughter Sophie brought me things from the outside, to lessen my insulation from the world. Dusty moths that covered her palm. Lizards, skittish and weak from their time in her hands. These things chilled me.

One morning she brought me a dead bat, which she

spread out on the glass table in the dining room. I was called in for a look.

"Jesus!" I shouted. "Wash your hands! Use Clorox!"

She was nineteen then, a sensible girl I thought.

"Stop it," Sophie said, walking to the edge of the table. She spit the words out in a way that made them impossible to ignore. "It's a big bat," she said, "when you stretch its wings."

I had taught her this, no doubt. The fascination with the lower forms. Later, without a word to Sophie, I wrapped the bat in a dry-cleaning bag and threw it in the garbage can out back. The last I saw of it were the words on the bag: "This is not a toy. Keep away from children." Ample warning. Something would eat it, I felt sure.

Sophie moved in with me two years after I left my wife Grace, although she was eighteen, plainly old enough to be on her own. Grace openly approved of Sophie's decision to come with me and I took this as a sign of faith in me, in the sort of guidance and support I could be expected to offer. Sophie and I had always relied on each other's company. When she was five, she spent three days laying out a patio with me in St. Petersburg. At first, she lugged the bricks to me, one at a time, pressing them up against her chest or cradling them in her arms. I set them in according to a pattern that Sophie herself had pointed out in a local shopping mall. Sometimes she rested on the stack of bricks and I brought her red, sugary drinks from the kitchen. Later, when her hands grew sore, she stopped carrying the bricks and simply stood next to me, stamping the bricks into place until we were finished.

It was a story that both Grace and I liked to tell again and again over the years. When the talk turned to teenagers,

I'd tell the brick story. "I don't worry too much about So-phie. When Sophie does things," I'd say, "she finishes them." Sometimes I'd hear Grace tell the same story at the end of a dinner, as the plates were lifted all around us. She drew none of my conclusions. "I watched the two of them from the kitchen," she would say. "They were very cute together. She didn't care at all about the patio, but she never left his side."

In Tallahassee Sophie kept her own hours and rarely told me where she went, or whom she knew. She took classes at the university. She waited tables. She was evasive about her life away from the house and I tried not to domineer. When we took walks after dinner, she liked to talk about the places we had been, the things we had seen together. The truth was I knew nothing about her life. I admired her need for privacy.

I liked having Sophie with me there because she seemed to know so much. She knew how to get rid of bedbugs, for instance. Where had she learned that kerosene-soaked rags, when slipped into the box springs, drove them away? I liked her soups, too. Where had she learned the soups?

As for my part, I pushed her to get a better job. I went on and on about staying in college. I fried the eggs in the morning. I slept in the living room, in the Murphy bed, the one where the bedbugs had lived. I believed that we were friends.

When she turned twenty, Sophie left. I had no idea where she went. She packed her things while I was at work and left the same day. There was a note taped to the center of the bedroom door. "Daddy, I'm not leaving you, but I am going. Love, So."

I called Grace, who reassured me. "She's okay." Over Grace's tinny voice I could hear my son Nick bouncing a basketball on the kitchen floor.

"Tell him I laid that floor," I said. "Tell him not to do that."

Grace ignored me. "She's with a perfectly nice family."

"Family? What do you mean family?"

"Give her some space," Grace said. Then she put her hand over the mouthpiece and said something to Nick. The bouncing of the ball on my former floor went on. I could hear it when she said to me, "She needs space."

In Sophie's bedroom there were scraps of paper, the beginnings of letters to people I didn't know. Tamara. Hubert. Mrs. Hartley. At first I tried to piece them together, hoping to draw out some clue as to where she might be. I spread them on the dining room table like a quilt.

"Dear Penny, I'm sure you won't want to hear this."

"Matthew, Try hard not to think your life to death."

"Howie—Get out of the restaurant business. Now."

Nothing came of this. They were just names, mostly first names, and no places or times were mentioned. She gave advice, I noted, and she rarely hedged.

I was working as a draftsman, taking contract work from a friend's office in Tallahassee. I often worked at home, on the sun porch. On Sundays I drove the finished drawings into the city and dropped them at the office. On the return trip I often stopped to buy a cigar and have breakfast. Sometimes I felt old and defeated, the victim of a routine. I decided not to fight the feeling. I went ahead and ate my eggs.

One Sunday, with the office empty as a wastebasket, I wanted a piece of pie and decided on my favorite spot, the Pelican Cafe. It had a driving range behind it. I thought I might hit a bucket.

It was twelve miles out there, so I lit up a cigar as I

drove. The interstate was deserted. Now and then the big trucks roared by. I hadn't seen Sophie in weeks. I reassured myself constantly. This was living in the dark, something you had to get used to.

When I turned off the ignition at the Pelican, I heard the familiar smack of golf balls over the noise of the kitchen fan. I could smell grease and freshly cut grass. I loved the farmers who hit at the driving range. They could really pop it; there was drama in their swings.

Inside I took a table and ordered an iced coffee and a piece of key lime. The place was nearly empty, save a guy thumbing an agricultural report at the counter. I stood to search for a spare newspaper and Sophie walked in. On the door, tiny bells rang.

I fought off the urge to go to her and returned to my table. Taking a mouthful of coffee, I sat and looked out the window at the red van. Sophie was thin and tan, her blond hair lighter than I remembered. She sat down across from me.

"I looked for you here last week," she said. "I know you're mad."

"Last week I came on Saturday," I said. The door of the van opened then and the driver got out. He was fat, very fat. He wore a blue velour sweatsuit and a beach hat pulled down over his long black hair. I had to ask. I had to hear it. "Who's that?"

Sophie smiled when she looked at him. "That's Joe," she said. "Joe Sport."

I felt myself wince. "That's his name?"

The pie came and Sophie nodded. She still tilted her head when she wanted me to understand. I took a forkful and kept my eye on her friend.

"He's a voodoo master," she said softly.

I took a bite. Sometimes life loomed too large. Here is

Sophie. Here is Joe Sport, voodoo master. Here is Dan Foley and his piece of pie.

I shook my head, thinking it purely a gesture of puzzlement. Sophie seemed to think I was angry. She reached across the table and touched the back of my hand. At that point Joe Sport leaned into the van and pulled out a big club.

"Your mother said he was a farmer." I didn't take my eyes off him.

"He is a farmer," she said. "But he travels too and he does the voodoo. I cook for him and look after his mother." She seemed so earnest I thought she might pop. Joe Sport took the club and banged on his right front hubcap until it clattered onto the pavement. Then he bent over and checked something on the wheel.

"Are you coming home?" I asked.

She took a fingerful of pie and put it in her mouth. "That's good," she said. "Not yet. I don't like the house. I don't feel anything there."

Now Joe Sport bent over, sweatsuit spread wide, and jabbed a pressure gauge into the valve of the tire. I looked at Sophie then. "Feel anything? What's not to feel?"

She took a deep breath and before she got a word out, I found myself asking, "What if I came to visit?"

She raised her eyebrows then. "I don't know. I'm not sure Joe would like it. He does a lot of secret things there."

I pushed the pie across to her. "Voodoo things?"

"Breeding," she said, pulling the plate close, reaching for my fork. I must have looked even more distressed because she laughed. "Cattle. Cross-breeding."

I took another look at Joe Sport, who scratched a line in the dirt with his club, then stared out at the driving range. Suddenly Sophie rose. "I work there, Daddy. It's my job."

"What if I follow you?" I said, completely sure that was the thing to do.

She smiled. "Joe might want me to hex you." She bent down and kissed me right on my temple. Probably a hex in itself.

"Hex?" I said. "Me? Hex your father?" But she was gone as quickly as she came.

I followed them through the farm country above Tallahassee. Soon they turned west and headed toward Alabama. The land rolled into thin woods, broken by long fields of alfalfa and soybeans. Occasionally I passed fields of cows, spreading like random toys. I calmed myself by smoking another cigar and listening to some dim gospel music on the radio.

Finally they turned onto a farm near the Alabama border. I gave some thought to driving straight by, more than I had to following them out there really. I could only guess why I was there. Instinct, I supposed. Sophie and I did things. We baked elaborate tortes together. We threw lawn darts at the raccoons together. We fought wars against the roaches together. I wanted that back.

I pulled in behind the van, drove down the dirt road toward a pair of white houses. Beyond that was a barn, to the right a wide field. Cows grazed in the distance. When the van stopped near the houses, so did I. Goats climbed the low branches of a twisted crab apple tree. In the tall grass by the side of the road I could see movement. Cats. They fanned out. I turned the ignition off. The radio still played. Even so, it seemed dead quiet. Underneath the music I could hear cat feet in the grass.

The passenger door opened and Sophie climbed out of the van. She waved to me and reached back in for a bag of groceries. I thought about helping her, but Joe Sport got out of the driver's side as I shifted in my seat. He just wobbled off ahead of Sophie, without so much as a glance at me, to the nearest house—the bigger one—which had a deck and a satellite dish. He held the door for her and they went in. Just like that.

I was pinching my teeth down on my cigar stub, when I heard Sophie's voice. She called to me from a tiny window on the second floor of the big house. I leaned across the front seat, but I couldn't hear her. "What?" I yelled and hit the radio.

"Doctor Joe says go to the little house." I got out of the car and Sophie shut the window as if it were part of the same motion. I straightened my tie and went for the door of the big house and knocked. I was trying to muster something: strength, anger, answers.

"Sophie!" I yelled. "Is he a doctor?" I wanted in.

I heard her voice close by, just behind the door. "Go to the little house, Daddy."

After that she wouldn't answer. The knob wouldn't turn, but I didn't panic. I had achieved a level of victory. I could come back. I could kick things in.

Despite the general hum of the insects, this didn't look like a voodoo yard. A muddy soccer ball lay up against the house, a pile of shovels near the air-conditioning unit. I heard Sophie's voice again. She was back in the little window, so that her face was all I could see. "We want you to stay for the party."

"What kind of party? Sophie, come out here." I found it discomforting to give her orders. It had been years. She didn't seem to hear. "A voodoo party?"

"Doctor Joe's mother is there," Sophie said. "She'll give you coffee."

"Is he a doctor? I thought he was a farmer."

"He's called Doctor Joe here," she said. She pulled back and shut the window.

It was too much. Maybe Sophie would come out if I

followed instructions. I decided that I would just stay there until she did. I walked to the little house and stood on the porch. I could wait there, keep an eye on things, piece some of this together.

Inside, an old woman was singing in a deep, rocky voice: "I walk on pins, I walk on needles, I walk on gilded splinters, I want to see what they can do." She opened the door before I could knock.

"It's you!" she said. She was tall, much bigger than she sounded, her hair wrapped in a green scarf. She had on overalls and a T-shirt that said TAMPA BANDITS.

"Yes," I said. There were cats all around my legs.

"You're Fooley. I know you, Fooley. Sophie showed me pictures."

It surprised me that Sophie had pictures, though it shouldn't have. She had taken most everything. I corrected her on my name, "Foley," I said. "Daniel Foley."

She turned, waved a wiry arm. "You can come in. I know you."

I could see through to the kitchen. The tables were covered with mason jars. On the floor just in front of me was a small stuffed animal. A bobcat. I stepped in.

"I expect you'll want coffee," she said. "Joe sends everyone over for coffee."

I nodded. She waved her arm again as she went into the kitchen. "Sit," she said. There were rocking chairs. I chose one. In the kitchen she sang: "They think they must frighten me, those people must be crazy, they don't see their misfortune or else they must be drunk."

Soon she came up behind me, lifting the cup of steaming coffee straight over my head. Everything around there was a dare, a test. Figure this. Now watch this. This'll really get you.

"My son was born in this house," she said as she bent down and sat.

The coffee was too hot to sip. I looked at her and said the first thing that came to mind. "How long is that now, Mrs. Sport?"

She raised her eyebrows until it looked like they hurt. Outside I heard the goats moving around that tree. "Why do you call me 'Sport'?" she said, hissing at me. "My name is Mrs. LaVelle. That boy changed *his* name, not mine. He left this house. He can change his name if he pleases. I'm still here and I ain't no damned 'sport.' "

I heard a tractor start a long ways from there. She was quiet for a minute before she poked out a bony finger. "Why are you here?"

I straightened up despite myself. "I followed Sophie here," I said. "I wanted to know where she lives."

"You don't know where your own daughter lives?" the old woman shouted. She was about to laugh.

"I didn't know," I said. "I do now." At that point I reached down and touched my car keys through my pant leg.

"You ain't answered my question! What did you come here for?" She shook her hand in front of my face.

I had come to get Sophie. "I thought maybe Sophie would come back," I said.

The old woman laughed at that. "What do you think? You think you're some 'venging angel, coming down here to snatch Sophie up?"

I shook my head and blew on my coffee.

"You think you're the Avenger?" she said, covering her mouth now, laughing. She kept on like that, laughing to herself, every once in a while saying loudly, "Fooley, the Avenger. Coming to bring us home. Yes sir. Old Fooley."

I said nothing. I wasn't sure what she thought was so funny. As a matter of fact, rescue was not out of the question.

We were quiet then. I knew I could sit right there until

Sophie came out. The old woman didn't seem to mind. Cats jumped in and out of the window. The woman talked on and off, about farming, or that house, and soon it seemed to me that she was just humming. I didn't talk. I watched the door and waited for Sophie.

Finally it began to get dark. The old woman got up and closed the windows. The lights went on in the big house. When I got up to say good-bye the old woman said, "We'll see you up at the party." I walked across her porch and through her tiny garden. I told myself I wasn't going to any voodoo party.

The sunset was just about over. Far out in the fields, beyond the house, I could see the cattle gathering. The sight of them made me stop. They were wrong, too wide and black in the distance, like no cows I had ever seen. Their heads rose from the middle of their backs into massive humps which, from that distance, looked like growths, tumors. Their jowls were enormous, their legs absurdly short.

I found myself walking past the house to get a look. The grass was deep, the soil sandy. My feet rose, fell, twisted back and forth and the light got worse as I stumbled forward. I bent down, squinted, cupped my hands at the side of my head like blinders, so that I could focus. I couldn't make connections. The closer I got to these things, the less sure I was of what they were. It felt dangerous.

Then, strangely, the party started. There was music in the big house, maybe a quarter of a mile behind me. I could see a silhouette dancing in a long window. How had that happened? How had I missed that?

When I turned back to the cows, I was sorry I had taken my eyes off them. It was too dark to see. They were shadows. I tripped forward, into a small bush that caught at my pant leg. I kicked and jerked until I fell into a loose spin that sent me whirling backward, my arms spread, ready to grab anything.

I hit the ground hard and lay there, my chest growing tighter. Rap music pulsed from the house. The dead grass and thistle formed a nest around me. At some point I closed my eyes. Soon I heard a small plane in the distance. I rubbed my face, then my arms and belly, and made no move to rise. Things were so tight, I began thinking heart attack.

I once saw Sophie like this in St. Petersburg, lying on our front lawn when I made the turn from the back of the house on my riding mower. She'd spread her arms wide, then wouldn't move. "Mow around me," she yelled. I could only read her lips over the blare of the engine. "Let me stay like this," she mouthed. But I waited until she stood and came to me before I put things in gear.

I rested there on my back—perhaps I slept—but however long it was, when I sat up the herd was all around me, shifting and turning above me. Slowly, sleepily. Truthfully, I had felt them moving in, first sensed them in the ground below me. Now they brushed and rumbled all around, stamping the grass near my hands.

These weren't cows. They were buffalo. Big, matted, stinking. The one next to me had this black, silver-dollar eye. He was sleeping.

Beside me I heard breathing and the occasional splash of urine in the soil. I was sick of mystery. I felt abused, in sore need of some help. But at the same time, I had the urge to start a stampede, to bust into the middle of that voodoo party, walk straight through the fires and the chicken blood, grab Sophie, throw her in the back seat of my car and go.

When I stood, they cleared and I wasn't scared of their weight anymore. The house was a distant place, light spilling from its windows. The Supremes were playing. The sound of horns, a brass section, came out across the grass, and faded out toward the buffalo behind me.

I felt exceptionally clearheaded. I was walking. Circling in. No one inside the house could see me out in the tall grass, but soon I could see into each room clearly.

It was no voodoo party. In one bedroom a tall guy in a blue blazer watched a basketball game on TV. In the other bedroom a woman brushed out her blond hair, while two kids jumped on a double bed, frantic with laughter. In the living room people milled back and forth carrying carrot sticks and tiny napkins. Matches flared, cigarettes were lit. In the corner a boy changed a record on the stereo. The music came through the plate glass in waves. I knew what this was. It was a cocktail party.

I went closer, climbed up on the deck. There was a sliding glass door on this side of the house. Sophie sat cross-legged on the floor next to the old woman, Mrs. LaVelle. The old woman reached down and stroked Sophie's hair. In the corner, wearing a wide red tie, was her son—Joe Sport, Doctor Joe, the voodoo master—talking to two short black women. He was freshly shaven, with rings on his fingers, his hair combed straight back from his forehead. He had an apron on.

Beneath the deck then I heard a goat bleating. I knelt down in the darkness to hear it more clearly. I could see nothing, but the call came again, frantic, insistent. I spread my hands on the planking, bent down to be closer.

The old woman saw me first. It was her voice I heard over the music, calling my name, my real name: "Foley! It's you!" I looked up from my hands and knees. Sophie waved and the whole party turned to look. I didn't move. Joe Sport rolled the glass door to one side and suddenly I smelled them all, close, smoky and familiar. "Come in," he said. "We were wondering about you."

Beneath me was a goat, an animal, a baby—trapped or being eaten, giving birth or burning. In front of me, my daughter, reaching out, beckoning me in from outside. I crouched low, said her name. I was ready for anything, even a mighty leap like this one.

Foley
the Great

F oley liked to remember the authority he'd had when he could say things and make them true. Sophie seemed to have that power now. He watched with admiration the way she devised new things to cook. She worked without recipes. "This would be good with scallions and yogurt," she could say of a particular soup, and it would be so.

When he was younger he seemed to have words inside him, welling up as he prepared to speak. Often what came out of his mouth surprised him—snatches of thoughts, full-blown sentences, sounds even. It was as if they had just grown there. Over time it proved dangerous.

Before their divorce, he was once in an argument with Grace, during which he said, "I wish you smoked cigarettes." They had been arguing about something small, like cleaning, and things had escalated quickly. Grace had been scowling at him, telling him what he was—lazy, tired, afraid—when he spit the words out at her. His only conscious hope had been that she would stop, that she would turn away. The sentiment made no sense at all to him; he felt that the sentence had been piped in from a long way off.

Grace understood right away. "Death," she said. "You want me to die."

Foley was stunned. "No, no, no," he said.

"What then?"

"No, no," Foley said, but suddenly there were no words. The connection from the outside had been cut. Now the cigarette line shocked even him. "I mean yes. I was implying that, I guess, but I didn't mean it."

Grace smiled. "You said it."

"I did," Foley said. "I know."

At that, Grace placed her hand on her chest. "Oh," she said. "You may be in luck." She coughed, lightly at first, then harder until she was heaving. She wheezed his name, reached for him.

"Come on," Foley said. "Stop." Grace gripped at her chest, rolled her eyes. "I'm sorry," he said. "I didn't mean it. Just stop."

He was laughing, as was she. It was like that. They could be deep in an argument, full of hurtful glances and meanness, and with a few words, stop, laugh, then turn from each other and go back to what they were doing—rewiring a lamp or boiling egg noodles. This tended to happen magically, Foley liked to think, as if some combination of words had tripped a switch somewhere.

As an old man, he could remember the first time he ate the sweet challah bread his mother bought at a delicatessen in Utica. He sat in a wedge of sunlight at the kitchen table, tearing the bread into tiny pieces, jamming them into his mouth wildly, without pause. His mother moved all around him, wiping down the counters with a stale-smelling dishrag. "Slow," she said. "Eat slow."

Foley took a dry swallow. "Best," he said, nodding,

stuffing another piece of the sweet bread into his mouth. "The best bread."

When he said that about the bread his mother smiled, nodded and sat down next to him, plainly taking notice. "I like it too," she said, leaning forward, grabbing a piece from his fingers. "In fact I love it. Your father doesn't much like it. But you're right, it *is* the best." She pushed the piece of bread into her mouth, then took another and another. They laughed, cheeks bulging. Foley chewed, pushed more bread in. He raised a fist and shook it for emphasis. "The best!"

He recognized that to be the first time he had said anything with authority. He was a little boy. No one listened to him. While he liked feeling that they were conspirators, holding a secret against the world, he loved the fact that he had said something—"This is the best bread!"—and it was suddenly true. He felt powerful. He—a kid, a boy, a nothing—had shown this truth to his mother. Yet when he tried to figure out where the thought had come from, he couldn't even remember thinking the bread was the best, only saying that it was so.

In the weeks that followed he tried out his new power. Once, after listening to a baseball game on the radio with his brother Hank, Foley said, "Johnny Roseboro is the best player ever." But Hank wasn't having any of it. "Are you out of your mind?" he said.

"He is," Foley said.

Hank squinted. "You dope."

"He is," Foley said, suddenly unsure of himself. He had calculated the statement for three innings, picking Roseboro because he hit a home run, then caught two runners stealing in the next inning. Foley let the words fly just as Hank clicked the radio off, even as the dial light dimmed and went out.

"Don't talk about what you don't know," Hank said, turning away from him, kneeling to thumb through their father's magazine rack. Foley could see the cover logos snapping by, again and again. LIFE. LIFE. LIFE. TIME. "What about DiMaggio?" Hank said. "There are hundreds of players, Dan. What about Duke Snider? What about pitchers? What about Bobby Feller?"

"Roseboro," Foley said. The name seemed to make him stronger. Foley shook his head. "Roseboro."

Hank laughed and that stung Foley, who kept his arms crossed in front of him. "You don't know anything, Dan," Hank said, pulling out a magazine. "Live and learn."

He tried it again and again in the coming weeks. "Pall Malls are the best!" he said to his father, who stopped tightening a bolt only long enough to say, "Have you been smoking, Dan?" Foley shook his head. "If you are, tell me, you'll be in trouble, but tell me."

"I haven't," Foley said. "I just think Pall Malls are the best." His father went back at the bolt. "They smell the best anyway," Foley said. He had no authority here. His father wasn't listening. "Pall Malls *smell* the best."

His father said nothing. Later Foley overheard him telling his mother, "Dan's been getting into the cigarettes. We'll have to start counting them."

That made Foley feel powerless, like a pet or a baby. His father had misunderstood. Foley sensed that what he had said about Pall Malls might be true, if his father would only listen.

When Foley turned sixty-three, Sophie wanted him to move to the farm, to retire. She came into the city to visit him in his office, where he worked one or two days a week. Her husband Joe and she both wanted it, she said. Joe's mother had recently died and Foley could have the small house to himself. There would be grandchildren soon.

Although he said no, Foley liked the idea of living with Sophie and working with Joe on the farm. He had grown fond of Joe after years of mistrusting him. Joe made claims to several lives, having lived at different times as a shrimper, a state trooper, a preacher. He had once owned a gun shop, he said, called Joe's Sport and Game, which he'd operated right out of his living room. Everyone, all his friends and neighbors, had shortened that name to Joe's Sport. Long after the gun shop was closed, people still referred to the farm as Joe's Sport. Soon many began to use that as Joe's name— Joe Sport—until Joe finally adopted it himself.

Foley loved the way Joe walked the land, showing him the animal dens, pointing out the snakes, kneeling to check the soybeans, revealing his plans. He'd wave his arm and say, "That's where we'll dig the next well" or "We'll dig a catfish pond there. You can show me how." He spoke inclusively, as if Foley were someone he was in business with, which was precisely what Foley mistrusted at first, mistakenly thinking that Joe was lining himself up for a loan. But Foley had learned that Joe made more on animal husbandry in one year than he himself now made in five.

Soon after Joe and Sophie were married, Joe had been banned from the local nursing home because he practiced healing without a license. "I can't even visit!" he said to Foley one morning over Sophie's lukewarm coffee. "They're my patients. They count on me." When Foley called the nursing home to straighten things out, the director said, "Your son-in-law is not quite a criminal, but he's getting there."

Foley tried to barter some design work in trade for letting Joe see his patients, but the director was firm. "Last time we let him in, Joe lit a fire in the hallway. He burned one woman's photographs," he said. "It took us forever to get the residents calmed, never mind all the smoke." When Foley confronted Joe with this, his son-in-law replied, "Her pneumonia's gone, isn't it?" Foley hadn't asked.

"What you do is illegal," Foley said. They were black-topping Joe's driveway. Using a crowbar, Joe bent back the lid of a great black barrel.

"I don't do anything," Joe said, dipping the crowbar into the black, murky liquid. It looked like something from the center of the earth.

"You don't do anything? Voodoo is something, isn't it? What about the people you heal?" Foley asked. "Sophie says you're a voodoo master."

"That's just some name she made up," Joe said. "Those people, they want me to help them. They believe I can do it, but they heal themselves."

"Voodoo," Foley said. He said it to hear if it sounded fake.

"My mother taught me some," Joe said. "But mostly I do whatever occurs to me. Songs, fire, blood. It's all the same. People like to think I have power, that I'm magic. I just let them go right ahead. No harm comes of it."

Foley loved his daughter. On the day she came to invite him to live with her, she dressed up—for the office, Foley knew, for the people he worked with. But her clothes were too loose, a bit faded; her purse was impossibly large and over-loaded. Although only thirty-one, she had begun to look old to him. Her skin seemed tight, but there were tiny crinkles in the corners of her eyes. Only a month before he had no-ticed how long, how rough with calluses, how unlike his own her hands were. She was a country woman now, he could see. Still, her movements—the way she adjusted things effortlessly, ran her fingers along flat surfaces when no one was watching—spoke to him of her happiness.

He could tell that she had practiced her argument, and he admired her for that. He was tempted to coach her as she made her case. Just say it, he wanted to tell her. Just open your mouth.

"You don't have any real work here," she said.

"This is work," Foley said, looking around his office. He walked to the drafting table, picked up a schematic. "I'm working here."

"You never see what you do," she said.

That was true. In Tallahassee he did contract work, some consulting, whipped out schematics and load-ratio reports. In the office, he was all business. Mostly he worked at home. He never visited sites and hadn't seen the need since he wasn't shepherding large projects. What was the last site he had visited? The medical arts building in Chiefland, early on in the project. All concrete and mud. What had he done there? Checked the pilings, sipped coffee. There had been small talk with the contractor. He jacked his car over a curb on the way out of the site.

"Everything I do is hidden," he said to Sophie. "It's electrical or air conditioning. It's all behind the walls." Even as he said this, he knew that she was right about his job, that she had hit on something when she said, "You never see what you do." From then on, it struck him as an absolute, as a truth Sophie had discovered when she said the very words. *You did it,* he wanted to say. *You said it. You have the power!*

Soon after, when Foley quit his job, he decided to travel to St. Petersburg to take stock of the things he had done when he was an architect proper. He might move back there, he figured, or out to the farm with Sophie and Joe. He wasn't making any real plans.

He made the drive in a morning, stopping only to chug down small bottles of grapefruit juice in gas station parking lots along the way. On the car seat next to him was a box of powdery doughnuts.

Pulling off Route 19 on the north side of the city, he felt that he was in an alien land. He recognized nothing. The curbs were all brand new—sharp, concrete moldings that rose up at the side of the road like levees. New parking lots lined the streets, signage rose up in shimmering walls, entire blocks of small businesses—locksmiths, paint shops, coffee shops—had been replaced by single gas stations.

When Nick was a boy, there was a tourist spot called Tiki Gardens, which Foley took him to from time to time. It was a Polynesian gift shop, fronting an elevated board-walk that ran through a large swamp. Foley took him there for no reason other than the quiet. Nick loved it because they had once seen an alligator there. One afternoon they saw a man have the tip of his finger bitten off by a snapping turtle. Nick thought the man was brave for reaching in the turtle's mouth. Foley said he was a fool. It was one of their first arguments. They stood six feet above the brackish wa-ter, a mile off the highway, and three feet from one another, holding hands. "Brave," Nick would say. "Stupid," Foley would shoot back. Nick, Foley realized on his return to St. Pete, was looking for the power.

Now Tiki Gardens was gone—the swamp filled and paved over, the exotic cypress road sign dismantled. The cafeteria where he and Grace had once taken the kids for cheap, vegetable-laden dinners was gone too, replaced by a giant store called FoodMax. The kite shop Nick had loved, the shell shop where Foley bought the blowfish that charmed his mother every Christmas, the theater where he had first met Grace, the angled side streets of Madeira Beach, all of these were missing or replaced.

Foley had expected this. Grace had told him about it for years. She had long since moved south to Fort Myers, where, she informed him, it was happening all over again. None of it really mattered to him. None of this was his work. He raced to his first stop, a bank on the inlet at John's Pass. A bank of his design. A bank he had made.

Since the divorce, Grace had taken to calling him Dan as most people did. Before that, she had called him by his last name. When people asked why she called him Foley, Grace had always answered, "That's how I've always known him."

Things around the house were always getting labeled along those lines. Foley's lamp. Foley's steaks. Foley's shoes. Foley's Chevy. He always saw this as correct, since they were a family. Each of them was a Foley; these things were theirs too. Foley's driveway. Foley's clothesline. Foley's plumbing.

When the kids were small, riding together in the back seat of the station wagon, they pointed to the buildings he had worked on. Sophie, pointing over Nick's shoulder: "There's Foley's mall." Nick, with ice in his mouth: "Dad's bank, Foley's bank."

Once, when they were all together, driving Gulf Boulevard with the sun cutting down between the beach houses, he decided to take them to a restaurant he liked. A beach place near the bridge to Treasure Island, where the special was always grouper sandwich and a glass of beer. In the parking lot, Grace balked. She saw it as seedy and refused to let him take the children inside. "It's a joint," she said, hands folded in her lap. "Those men play pool for money." He and Grace were in the front seat, staring at the milling shadows in the windows. This stung Foley, although he couldn't say why. He could think of no way to respond, but found himself speaking anyway. "That's not so bad. I play pool for money all the time."

Grace squinted. In the back seat, Nick and Sophie plainly perked up. "Oh, come on," Grace said. "I've never seen you so much as touch a pool rack."

"You mean stick," Foley said.

"Or cue," Nick piped in.

At that point, it was up to Foley to qualify the statement. He could back off, he knew. Claim it as overstatement, but hang with the premise. *He had played for money,* he could say, *when he was younger.* But he stuck fast to his story.

"I do," he said. "I do." He wanted them to go inside. He could show them something about him they never knew, something they had never seen before, some talent he had yet to discover. He could really concentrate, make one serious run on any table. That could happen anytime.

"So what are you now, Foley?" Grace said. "A pool shark?"

Nick loved that. "Foley the pool shark!"

Sophie leaned forward, put a hand on his shoulder. "Yeah, Foley the pool *king!*" she said.

"Minnesota Foley," Grace said, softly laughing.

"Super Foley!" Nick said, lurching forward, throwing a fist out in front of him. "Foley the Great!" Sophie shouted. "Foley the Great!"

Foley turned to Grace, who was watching the frenzy, laughing, and then started the car. "Oh come on!" Nick shouted. "Let's play!" Sophie echoed him. "Let's play pool!" Now it was a chaos of jumping and cheering and hands slapping upholstery. But the kids weren't frantic about it and didn't whine when Foley backed up and said, "No, no. Your mother's right. That's not our life." They merely kept on with the cheering, leaned forward to their parents, naming and renaming their father all the way home.

After that even his own children called him Foley from time to time. Late in the evening, Nick would shuffle into the kitchen with a schoolbook in hand, just after Foley had wiped down every counter. "Foley," he would say, "math bites." And Foley would sit with him and work through problem after problem at their soap-smelling table, without correcting him, without reclaiming the name Dad, as that was a different Foley—*Foley the Dad*. When Nick came to him for help like this, he was *Foley the Problem Solver*. It was the same thing for Sophie, who called him Foley in a regular, patterned way, when he was far away—on a trip or when, after the divorce, he'd phone them from Tallahassee. *Foley the Absent. Foley the Missing.*

They never called him Foley in front of anyone else, and rarely in front of their mother. Once when he was calling home from Los Angeles, Grace handed the receiver over to Sophie, who said, "Is this Foley?" In the background Foley heard Grace correct Sophie. "Daddy," she said. "Call him Daddy."

When Grace got back on the phone, Foley said that he didn't mind, that he sort of liked it.

"Well, I don't."

"It's only a name," Foley said.

"To her you're Daddy," Grace said. "You're her Daddy."

"Either way," he said, "I'm still her Daddy."

Grace sighed. "Foley is your name. That's all. Anyone can call you that."

*   *   *

It took Foley a while to find the bank he had come to see. He'd had to stop for directions at a gas station where the attendant sat in a glass booth surrounded by open cartons of cigarettes. He spoke to Foley through a microphone. "Just pump," he said as Foley approached.

"Excuse me?"

The attendant shifted the book in his lap and pointed to the pumps. "They're on," he said into the microphone. "You can pump."

Foley shook his head. "I need to know where the First American Bank is," he said too loudly. The light on the corner changed; the traffic sounds picked up.

The attendant touched his hand to his glasses and scanned the horizon, which from what Foley could see was all mall, interspersed with snatches of an inlet. Once he had walked this very ground, right here, where the giant gas tanks were now buried under all this cement, and kicked at lizards and deadwood. He'd carried a clipboard then. Workers milled nearby. Bulldozers waited for his command. Foley the Great. "Do you mean that little black bank?" the attendant said finally, after he'd looked full circle like an owl. Foley nodded. "It's over behind the Captain's Galley," the attendant said, pointing west, toward a strip mall.

"Is that a restaurant?" Foley said, squinting in the light.

"It's that boat behind the mall. See the masts?" Foley could. "It's a real boat," the attendant said. "They brought it right up on land."

There had been careful planning in the placement of this bank. It had been close to the main road, visible from the bridge. Years before, Grace had always pointed the bank out to the kids—"Foley's bank"—until they picked up on it and sang it out every time they saw it. Foley had heard it called that so many times he'd almost asked them to stop. He'd had a checking account there, a safety deposit box. But something had moved since then and he couldn't be sure what it was. The bridge maybe, or the road to the bridge. Everything had spread and turned and the bank had been displaced.

The attendant spoke. "You can't see the bank from here," he said. "Just scoot around the boat and it's right there. You can't miss it."

Foley raised a hand in thanks and walked to his car. The attendant leaned forward and, with his lips almost on the microphone, said "Bless you" so loudly that Foley jumped. When he turned back, the attendant was reading, caught deep in the middle of a page.

The sight of the bank was no disappointment to Foley. He watched for a while from behind the wheel of his car. It looked much the way he had drawn it in the plans, with the bank facing the back of the giant boat. The large grassy lot he'd planned had been eaten into by parking and the trees had long since been squeezed out, but otherwise things seemed in order, moving somehow according to plan.

A woman carried a cash bag from her car to the walk-up teller and that, Foley realized, was how he had drawn it up. He had planned on comings and goings, daily movements, patterns of traffic.

He got out of the car and locked the door. For the moment, he wanted to be in the flow. He walked inside, opened a savings account. There were handshakes, introductions, explanations. He cashed a check. Once that was done, he noted the wear of the floor marble, then went outside and sat on a cement bench, waiting out the dense heat of the afternoon. From there he caught glimpses of the inlet, and since mall and giant boat muffled the traffic noise, it was easy for him to remain there all afternoon.

When the tellers gathered at the end of the day, they left all at once. The last one out trailed a little, snapping her purse, sliding on her sunglasses. She stopped at the bench. "We're closed," she said.

"I know," Foley said, looking up at her. She looked out at her friends, who were unlocking their cars, some of them starting up, and then back to him. Foley stood. He was hot, stiff, a little dizzy, and probably red-faced, he knew. He smiled to let her know he was okay. She touched his arm. "Can I help you?"

He gave her the answer he had planned. He told her his name. Then he told her who he was and what he had done.

A NOTE ON THE TYPE

The text of this book was set in Bembo, a facsimile of a typeface cut by one of the most celebrated goldsmiths of his time, Francesco Griffo, for Aldus Manutius, the Venetian printer, in 1495. The face was named for Pietro Bembo, the author of the small treatise entitled *De Aetna* in which it first appeared. Through the research of Stanley Morison, it is now acknowledged that all old-face type designs up to the time of William Caslon can be traced to the Bembo cut.

The present-day version of Bembo was introduced by the Monotype Corporation, London, in 1929. Sturdy, well balanced, and finely proportioned, Bembo is a face of rare beauty and great legibility in all of its sizes.

Composed by Creative Graphics, Inc.,
Allentown, Pennsylvania

Printed and bound by Fairfield Graphics,
Fairfield, Pennsylvania

Designed by Cassandra J. Pappas